The Catalyst

Chris Reher

Chris Reher

By Chris Reher

Sky Hunter

The Catalyst

Only Human

Rebel Alliances

Delphi Promised

Quantum Tangle

Terminus Shift

Entropy's End

also available in eBook and audio format

ACKNOWLEDGMENTS

Thank You to Mallory Moutinho for
keeping that glass half full!
Also to Tracy Leach and Andy Brokaw

ONE

The only option now was to hide. No time to think, no time to regroup, no time to reach under her cumbersome skirt to retrieve the gun strapped to her thigh. The box in her arms seemed to grow heavier with every step and whatever sloshed around in there didn't make it any easier to deal with the ship's already sub-par gravity.

Nova Whiteside halted at a juncture where the main hall split into what appeared to be service passages. The carrier was mainly a cargo scow - surely some shipping container or supply closet down here would let her hide the box and get her bearings before someone else decided to shoot.

She chose one of the passages for no particular reason and pushed onward, aware that her arms were growing weaker and her shoulders seemed ready to pop a joint or two. She would have to put this thing down, and soon.

She elbowed a key plate to her left and laughed tensely when she found the door unlocked. It opened upon a narrow platform with a few steps leading down into a payload area crammed with cargo bins. She set the box onto a wheeled cart with a groan of relief.

The Myrid creature in the tank thrashed around in its cloudy matrix, agitated by the commotion that had started when their ship was boarded. The crew had just prepared the

Dyona's decks for the subspace leap toward Magra when four cruisers had overtaken them, only moments from the jumpsite. Their demands were simple: Stand and deliver, the call of pirates over millennia and in all corners of the galaxy. No commercial carrier stood to make profit by being destroyed and her captain had surrendered almost at once. Nova cursed him and his descendants. He had of course no idea what he was shipping out from Pelion but she felt better for having cursed him, anyway. She didn't know, either, but one didn't ask for an escort of seven armed and disguised Air Command soldiers to transport a pet.

Nova leaned over the platform railing to see no exits below other than a massive loading door. Nowhere to hide the box and no way to hide herself. She peered at the frightened Myrid through the glass. Could she leave it here? Who would want to harm such an inoffensive individual securely sealed in a tank? If she stayed they were both trapped and, if anything, she would only draw attention to it.

The mollusk had been serene and nearly immobile during the hours that Nova and her team had guarded it, shifting only when someone moved nearby. Now it seemed to want to break out of its confines and escape as badly as Nova did.

She went back to the door and found her decision made for her. "Damn!"

Voices in the hall. Rough talk, curses, shouts. And then they stopped.

"Lights zero," she whispered, using a common trade language. The ship's sensors obeyed and the room plunged into absolute dark. She leaned against the wall beside the door and fumbled under the long, multi-layered skirt to draw her gun. Her labored breathing sounded dangerously loud in this otherwise silent room and she fought to calm it.

"She's in here," someone said in heavily accented Centauri. "Look at that heat signature."

"I like 'em hot like that," another man replied and then the door sprang open, followed by the boot that had kicked it.

Nova leaped aside, her gun raised. She fired at the bright rectangle of light spilling from the hall, aiming at the silhouettes outlined there. One of them dropped to the floor. The other slipped into the shadows. She lost sight of him when the third man retreated into the hall, leaving her blinded by its light. A fist came out of the dark and caught the side of her head and she stumbled back, stunned by the blow.

"Lights!" someone shouted.

Nova looked up into the face of a Centauri pirate of considerable size who didn't seem too concerned about possibly breaking a few fingers in wrenching her gun away from her. Her hands, still weakened from the strain of carrying the tank, released it.

"The girl has some fight in her," he said. He turned and shouted into the hall. "Did you run away, Briggs?"

The other man, a Human, came back into the room. He grinned and closed the door behind him when he saw Nova. "Finally something worthwhile on this bucket of bolts."

Nova tore out of the Centauri's grasp and backed away. When the pirate followed he stumbled over the corpse on the floor. He looked at it and then at her, anger now clear on his face. "You did that, bitch?" He struck her with the back of his fist. Nova reeled backward and collided with the trolley that held the Myrid's container. She tried to reach for it but the cart slammed into the platform railing and she, and the box, tumbled over it and into the cargo area below.

Nova landed hard beside the tank. It had not shattered on impact but its lid had cracked and the corner gaped. Something began to leak from it. She was slow to gather herself and the two pirates vaulted the railing and dropped from above before she was able to get up.

"What, by the ghosts of Niedra, is that?" They could all see the Myrid's undulating limbs writhe frantically in the murky, yellowish fluid. The Human crouched to tap the tank and then leaped back with a surprised squawk when a large, bulbous eye swam out of the amber substance to slide along the glass.

His companion laughed. "Scared you, Briggs?"

The pirate kicked the tank as if to punish the creature within it. Still, it did not break. He stomped on it again as if its passive resistance meant a personal affront.

"Stop it!" Nova yelled. "What are you doing?"

"Shut up." He aimed his weapon at the container. "Let's take a look at that thing." He fired his gun several times until, at last, the lid of the tank melted and sprang open. A surge of fluid oozed over the floor, carrying with it the amber-colored Myrid.

Still sprawled on the floor beside the tank, Nova was unprepared when the creature slid toward her with surprising speed and wrapped its long limbs around her arms. The substance inside the tank seemed to be a very fine powder that sifted through these limbs like oil and made them just as slippery. There was no moisture and, as Nova watched in disbelief, some of the powder dissolved into the air.

Then one of the boneless limbs wrapped around her neck. She gasped when it tightened and a searing pain dug deep into her skin. Every muscle went rigid; she was unable to move, unable to pull the creature away. An intense heat spread from her neck throughout her body.

It was gone just as suddenly. The pirate had used his gun to push the Myrid away and then his heavy boot to crush it against the metal floor. To be sure, he raised his pistol and shot it several times. Nova slumped once released from the strange seizure, her hand pressed to her neck.

"Now I saved the Human's life." The Centauri gripped her arm to haul her to her feet. "You be sure to thank me nicely."

His companion coughed. "Let's get her back to the others. This stuff is making my throat itch."

* * *

Nova's resistance to being manhandled along the cargo ship's corridors and back to the main concourse was little more than a token gesture. The sting on her neck radiated excruciating pain and some sort of fog encroached upon the edges of her vision. She registered the scattered bodies of her fellow travelers with only passing interest. Her captor pushed her along a hallway where some of the other passengers huddled in dread, lined up against the walls. Pirates guarded them, guns drawn and heavy boots ready to kick those who dared to move from their spot.

Any interstellar journey dealt with the threat of pirates as part of the hazards, especially in rebel-dominated territory like the Pelion sub-sector. A successful journey was a matter of odds and firepower. But piracy existed for profit, perhaps to collect slaves or to confiscate vessels. Rarely did attacks result in the sort of carnage she had seen here today. Usually, passengers of no interest to the pirates were let go with their ship or dropped off elsewhere.

Nova touched her neck and then examined her hand. Blood, certainly, and also the powdered substance that had filled the tank. Her skin burned as if branded and the inside of her nose felt raw.

She sat on the floor between a woman whose weeping soon grated at her nerves and a man who stared listlessly at nothing. Settlers, merchants, smugglers, runaways and petty thieves. No one here was on vacation. She caught the eye of Lieutenant Nolas sitting along the opposite wall and raised her eyebrows in question. He lifted four fingers and then brushed them across his throat. Four of her squad members dead. That left her, Nolas and one other. She raised three fingers and wiggled one of them. He shrugged. He had no idea where the missing one was.

They both turned their heads when raised voices traveled along the corridor. The pirates moved among the passengers and crew, jabbing at some, cursing at others. A dozen or more of the captives were hauled to their feet and led toward the docking ports. Among them were a few handsome women, one or two crew members and two children. Nova and Nolas exchanged glances when the pirates selected a blue-haired man and shoved him after the others. The Delphian made no move to defend himself, apparently resigned to his fate.

Nova peered past them down the hallway to see a handful of pirates standing by a prone body. One of them wore a respirator tied over the lower part of his face.

"Why are you killing passengers?" he snapped, his voice muffled. "Did Gwain order that?"

"He said to take out the armed ones. We lost four of ours. Were we supposed to let them pick us off one by one?"

"Leave the rest alone. Where is the box?"

"With the slimy powder in it? Got smashed."

The masked man muttered a string of profanities. He stooped to turn the dead man onto his back and looked through his clothing until he found a communication device. "Union soldier." He straightened up and turned toward the rows of captives. "Any more of them?"

"None in uniform, so who knows."

Nova turned abruptly when one of the armed men loomed over her. His boot nudged her leg. "Here's a pretty thing." Rough hands pulled her to her feet and then she felt those hands move over her body in search of weapons. She glared at the Human but said nothing. Resistance was as likely to excite someone like him as it was to enrage. Neither toss of the dice would increase her chances of escape. Her hand moved to her back and slipped into the waistband of her skirt until she felt the handle of the knife that was secreted there. She would not give it up so easily, either.

"I'll take this one," a low voice intruded upon the thug's inspection. Nova looked up to see the pirate with the respirator. The eyes above the mask glowed with a violet luminescence as they reflected the overhead lights, marking him as a Centauri. The neural interface node at his temple identified him as pilot and was only partially hidden by loose waves of black hair.

"When I'm done with her."

The Centauri reached out to grasp a handful of Nova's

hair and pulled her toward himself. He released his mask for a moment as if to adjust it. Nova gasped. He nodded and replaced the respirator.

"Let her be," someone called out behind them. Lieutenant Nolas had come to his feet and strode toward them, looking ready to take them all on at once. The pirate who had groped Nova pulled his gun and leveled it at the lieutenant.

"You want to sit down in a hurry," he said. Nolas halted.

"Do as he says," the Centauri advised. He put his hand on the pirate's arm to push the gun aside. "I'll take the redhead with me," he said to him. "I think Gwain will like this one. Let the others go. We came for the damn tank, not a bunch of migrants."

Nova stumbled along with the Centauri, fighting the hand twisted in her hair. He hurried along the concourse, away from the pirates loitering there, and into a lounge near the locks where the enemy ships had docked.

He released her once out of sight of the others. Looking around, he strode to a bulkhead and used his gun to smash the lock on a box of emergency supplies. He found a respirator and handed it to Nova.

She stood in the middle of the room, wondering if the blow to the head she had taken earlier was affecting her in strange ways. She still felt dizzy but was she now also hallucinating? "What the hell is going on?"

"Put that on, Nova." He went back to the door and looked out into the hall. "We have to get out of here."

She slipped the mask over her face. "I said: What the hell is going on, Seth?"

He grinned. "Didn't expect to see me after all these years, Sweets? Get rid of your jacket."

"Why?"

"Because that powder on your clothes is the same that is going to be seeping through the entire ventilation system any moment now. How much of it did you breathe in?"

"A lot. It's making my throat hurt." She stepped out of

her skirt. She was glad to be rid of the disguise. Beneath the skirt and loose jacket she wore tight gray breeches, solid boots and a brief leather vest over a long-sleeved shirt. She gathered and tied her long hair at the nape. "Is it dangerous?"

"Very. Lean forward."

"What—"

"Do it!" He grasped her neck to bend her down and squirted her neck and chest with a bottle of saline he had pulled from the medicine cabinet. She sputtered when it ran into her respirator and fought his grip when the liquid burned her open wound. The floor below her turned pink.

He pulled her back up. "Sorry about that, but we're in a hurry." He handed her a wad of clean cloth to place over the wound on her neck. He taped it to her skin with absentminded efficiency before striding back to the door. "We're going to make our way down to lock four. They won't follow."

"Who, your pirate pals?"

"Not my pals," he said, again looking out into the hall. He grasped her arm and dragged her outside. They raced toward the docks, meeting no one.

"What about the others?" she protested and tried to slow down. His iron grip on her arm was unyielding. "I've got two other squad members here. And there are civilians. We can't just leave them!"

"No choice, Nova. Come on." He pulled her along. "The air here is poison."

"How do you know it's poisoned?"

"The tank broke?"

"What? Yes, it broke."

"Then the air is poisoned."

"We've got to warn them! There's got to be portable air on board. Order your people to take the passengers off the ship."

He hesitated. "They don't take orders from me."

"Try anyway! They can just dump them back on Pelion.

We're not that far."

He shook his head in resignation and they turned to run back up the main concourse where they had left the others. Both of them came to a sudden stop when they rounded a bend. People, both pirates and passengers, were stumbling along without direction, gasping in the caustic air now moving through the ship's conduits. They watched some of them drop, clutching their throats. A woman nearby saw Nova and raised her arms toward her, pleading silently for help.

"Too late. Let's go." Seth whipped her about and they hurried back to the freighter's docking ports. Once there, he propelled her into the airlock and closed the gate. "Nova, meet the *Dutchman*."

She released the opposite door and entered his ship through the umbilical.

"Where are we going?"

"Out of here. Sit down." Once through the cargo area, Seth crossed the untidy main cabin and stepped down into the cockpit. The *Dutchman*, a small private cruiser, whined into readiness. He barely waited for Nova to drop into the co-pilot seat before tearing away from the freighter, warning lights flashing their protest when her thrusters pushed it away from the larger ship's hull. They raced away, toward the jumpsite beacons.

Nova looked over the cockpit indicators. His acceleration exceeded anything she would have expected from a ship of this size. The crossdrive interface did not look like the design she'd expect on a private ship, either. Above them, a concave hologram wrapped the ship's immediate surroundings around them as both pilot benches tilted back.

"Ten seconds to the site," Seth snapped at her and connected the neural node at his temples to the ship's processors. When she did not reply he slammed his fist against a lever above her head. The crash guard came down hard on her collarbones.

She closed her eyes and steeled herself against the free-fall through subspace. The beacons responded to Seth's signal and the gate activated, opening to swallow them whole. Ships of any size entered such breaches through the power of complex calculation and survived by the strength of their shielding but a highly trained, sentient mind was needed to find the way out again. Not everyone possessed such a mind. Sometimes that exit remained elusive and over time ships were lost or disintegrated when they emerged at their destination. The body count went down when guide beacons were placed at Trans-Targon's busier sites, allowing lesser-skilled navigators to make the traverse safely. Acting as gateways to other sectors, these sites also allowed for the monitoring of traffic, a blessing or a curse, depending on who came to use them.

There was a long, silent moment of nothingness. No light, no sound, nothing resembled the tangible reality they had just left, now many light years away. This was a long jump, reaching from Pelion all the way to Magra Gate. But the span was well-charted and the *Dutchman* crashed back into normal space just as Nova started to wonder about Seth's navigation.

He slowed the ship and began a systems check. "Not a bad jump. I just about drained my coolants, though. We'll have to land on Aikhor." He disengaged his mental connection to the ship's processors and set the autopilot.

Nova stumbled out of the cockpit into the main cabin, a cluttered combination of living and work space, lined with storage bins and what appeared to be laundry. She tossed her respirator aside and slumped into a scuffed bucket chair. The dizziness had subsided but the happenings of the past hour had taken their toll. An annoying scrape in her throat demanded attention as much as the wound on her neck.

Seth followed and perched on the edge of a broad lounger beside her chair. "What a ride, huh? Does your neck hurt? It's still bleeding."

She leaned toward him and pulled his gun from its holster. She regarded it thoughtfully and then pointed it at him. The safety went off audibly enough. His eyes widened.

"I will give you about five minutes to explain why you attacked our ship and killed six Union officers along with over forty civilians and the crew. Not to mention how you knew about the tank and its contents. Then you are going to set course for Targon or I will kill you now and go there by myself."

Seth swallowed hard. Nova's accusation had been delivered with all the emotional involvement of a weather report. The barrel of the gun was aimed levelly at this head. He knew well that she was not only authorized but also quite capable of using it to kill even him.

TWO

"Put that away, Nova. You need me to fly this ship."

"I'm every bit the pilot you are. Don't think I didn't notice your crossdrives. That update isn't even available outside the military yet."

He glanced toward the cockpit. "You saw that, huh? Look, you're not about to shoot me. You can't fly this plane, navigate, and keep that thing pointed at me all at the same time."

"All the more reason to shoot you now. Is that what you are these days? A pirate?"

"No one was supposed to get hurt."

Her eyes narrowed. "You know, I don't think you'd bother with pirates, Sethran Kada. That's just too crude for you. But you are known to consort with rebels. I've heard about you over the past few years. Not a lot of commendable stuff."

"Oh? What have you heard?"

"You've raised hell in a bunch of places that'll never invite you back. Did some mercenary work, played the hero on Callas for a while. You have a habit of turning up where nasty things happen. Your name comes up when Tharron's favorite deputies get mentioned. You got arrested for smuggling dope and guns more than once. You are a wanted criminal in a lot of places."

He drew a knee up to wrap his arms around it, clearly measuring the distance from his not so relaxed body to her gun. He saw her watching him and smiled innocently. "I don't smuggle dope. Are you writing a memoir about me?"

"Air Command is."

"Sounds like they need a new hobby. I'm a small-time privateer compared to what's going on out here. You won't even get a pat on the back for turning me in."

"Privateer? Those people back there are dead because of you! Union agents shot. Others on their way to some slaver or to be ransomed if they're really lucky. That is treason, not small-time fun for profit!"

"Treason? I don't remember pledging allegiance to anyone lately. And if those cowboys of yours hadn't decided to start shooting they'd still be alive."

"Some of those cowboys were my friends. Why did you take me with you?"

He shrugged. "I couldn't let a woman–"

"There were two dozen other women aboard. Don't patronize me!"

"Well, maybe I wouldn't have taken you with me if I'd remembered what a handful you can be." He smiled disarmingly. It didn't work. "Since you know all about me, let's talk about you. But put the gun down, will you? It's got a touchy trigger."

Nova studied his lazy pose for a moment, knowing very well that he would uncoil and snap up her gun the moment she set it aside. Instead, she lowered the weapon without removing her finger from its trigger.

"Thank you," he said. "I have to say this is a fine welcome for an old friend. Will you not give us a kiss to say hello?"

"We were never friends."

"I recall differently. I was a virgin before I met you, I swear."

"Yah, right."

He smirked. "Last time I saw you, you were pointing

your academy pistols at anything that moved. I see they give you real guns now, First Lieutenant Nova Whiteside."

"You're familiar with my record also. I kinda like mine better."

"You've climbed the ranks over the years."

She tilted her head, unable to restrain her curiosity about what had brought them together in this strange circumstance. "It's been a while since you quit, hasn't it?"

"Six years." He leered at her. "You've grown up."

Nova's hand strayed to her already tightly buttoned collar. "And you've grown even more disrespectful."

He leaned forward, uncomfortably close. "Is there anything nice forthcoming here? Like: 'Hello, Seth, good to see you'. Something like that?"

She tipped her gun up until he sat back again, at a safer distance. "How about 'Hello, Seth, how come you left the base without notice or good bye?'"

"Oh. That."

"Yes, that."

He shrugged and looked at his hands. "I just had to get out of there. Too many rules. I couldn't keep them all straight in my head. So I jumped. They couldn't teach me anything else."

"That's just it! You were brilliant in every way. At the top of your tier all the time until you screwed up."

"You weren't so bad yourself, love."

"I am not trying to flatter you! You could have joined Air Command, too. We could have used you. Instead, you are a bloody pirate!"

"Stop ranting, Red. This is your life, not mine. If I couldn't make it through that academy, how do you think I'd handle military? I was never meant to be a soldier." He raised his hands away from his body. "Look, I'm going back there and get you some bandages. You're bleeding all over my nice chair. Don't shoot me - I'm not about to jump out of the airlock to get away from you."

She rolled her eyes and gestured with the gun. He rose

with fluid grace and she watched him walk toward the rear of the cabin to search through some bins. He wore comfortably shabby leather trousers and a loose shirt, looking every bit the pirate. His lithe body had changed little in the years since she had last seen it. In her bed. On the day when, after a long shift of maneuvers and exercise, she had returned to the base to find him gone.

They both trained under the same instructors, not far from graduating from Air Command's advanced flight training while pursuing additional studies. Seth had an intuitive understanding of people and retained entire volumes of histories, languages and customs of the worlds he studied. Her own interests leaned toward weapons and navigation. Their shared passion for aviation was boundless.

She had at first been taken by his looks. His effortless grace, so different from the awkwardness of her Human friends, was not easy to ignore. Although genetically nearly identical to her own species, there was still something sleekly alien about his people that fascinated her. There was no wasted movement, no incomplete gesture. The apparent laziness of his fine-tuned body belied the fact that he could strike like a snow cobra when moved to do so. It served him well and he often took over instruction for hand-to-hand combat training.

That Seth had been older than her classmates and also worked as a tutor while completing his advanced standing made him even more attractive to Nova. She had grown up on one military installation after another while her parents were assigned to wherever the need was greatest. Their only child was always closely guarded, always under the stern eye of her father who made it clear that a dalliance with another pilot, especially one who was not Human, would not be tolerated. The disciplines he had instilled in her were not easily left behind even after she set out on her own.

But neither her father's principles nor the academy's rules deterred her when Seth had singled her out. He demanded nothing from her but her company until she came to him.

Her experience with men had been limited to furtive groping among classmates and short-lived infatuations with seniors whose interest was fleeting and rarely extended beyond the bedroom. Seth had been her first real lover and made their encounters a series of joyful discoveries, unhurried and memorable. Weeks passed blissfully as they carried out their affair while eluding the watchful eye of supervisors and the ever-present security cameras.

It didn't last. Discipline did not come easily to Seth and he chafed under the daily routines to which they were subjected. His aversion to authority was decidedly at odds with the regimented career that Nova had chosen. Eventually, it was assumed, either Seth or the administrative body of the academy decided to terminate his training there.

She had missed him, then loathed him and then missed him some more. It took a while before rumors settled and she was able to put him out of her mind. Since then she had accepted one tour of duty after another, honing her skills, becoming a Hunter Class pilot and doing her part to help rid the Trans-Targon sector of an increasingly bold and dangerous rebel force. She had learned not to look back, on anything.

"Are you all right?" Seth intruded upon her memories. "You seem tired." He sat back down and opened a box of medical supplies. She pulled away when he reached for the crude bandage on her neck. "Oh, hold still," he said. "You're the one with the gun."

She took a deep breath, engaged the safety on the weapon and tossed it aside, onto the lounger. He was right - she wasn't about to shoot him and probably wasn't equipped to take his ship by herself through this rebel-infested sub-sector.

Seth grinned but said nothing when he turned his attention to her wound. He winced when she let him remove the patch. "That thing looks nasty."

She watched him while he applied disinfectant, too aware of his hands close to her body. A wide scar above his right eye had happened at some point during the past years but she seemed to remember every contour of his face as if she had seen it just yesterday. When his lips formed into a teasing smile she realized that he had caught her staring. The oddly glowing Centauri eyes were now watching her as intensely. "Are you sure you don't feel sick from breathing in that powder from the tank?"

She gathered herself. "Not very much. I'll be fine. Not as dangerous as you think it is, I guess."

His hands halted their task of taping a fresh gauze pad to her neck. "Nova, that stuff was almost fifty percent water ash. Didn't anyone tell you that?"

She gaped at him, speechless.

"See, now this is why I didn't join your tin soldier army. Let me guess. Your CO tells you to go under cover as the type of riff-raff that hangs around on Pelion and transport a ridiculously flimsy box containing some sort of cephalopod out of rebel territory. Of course no one tells you that the stuff it lives in is poisonous enough to annihilate an entire town if it got out into the air. But you accept the order, without question, because that's what you're told to do."

"That's my job," she hissed and pushed his hands away. "It's what I do."

"It's a witless way to live your life. And short."

"Not as witless as being a pirate."

"At least I have a choice."

"And how did you choose this one?"

He shrugged. "We were paid to capture your ship, retrieve the box and take it to Feyd. That's all. Wasn't meant to be that difficult."

"So that's your life now? Being a pirate? Looting rust buckets like that garbage scow for profit?"

"A man's got to eat, Babe."

"Don't call me that." She stood up and paced about the small cabin. "Who hired you?"

He propped a leg onto the armrest of her chair. "Why would I tell you that? At this point the best you can hope for is for me to drop you off some place nice where your people can find you. And for that you should be grateful, not ask me questions about things that don't concern you."

She rounded on him. "I am a Union agent! You attacked an Air Command operation. This concerns me deeply."

"So are you going to arrest me again, then? I find this confusing, seeing how I'm the one who kidnapped you."

Nova scowled, knowing that nothing she could say would ruffle him or move him to tell her anything he did not want her to know. She turned away, suddenly utterly fatigued and defeated. She and her team members had failed in their duty to protect the Myrid in the tank. Her colleagues, chosen for this detail only because they had been deployed on a base conveniently located to Pelion's jumpsite, were dead. She herself would be dead or a hostage now if not for Seth. And he knew it.

"Let's not do this," he said, replacing the mocking tone of his voice with something softer. "I'll drop you off on Magra. You can make your way to the Air Command base there but you know I'll be long gone before you can get anyone to come looking for me. It's a much better deal than what you would have gotten back on that transport."

She shrugged, but he was right and denying that would just sound foolish.

He stood up. "But first I have to pick up some coolant and get repairs done on Aikhor. Why don't you get off your feet for a while? You can take the crew cabin. I usually flop out here anyway. Just don't shoot me for a traitor while I sleep."

* * *

The *Dutchman* brooded quietly, its cockpit in darkness, the autopilot taking care of the next destination with silent efficiency.

Nova had retreated into the cramped crew cabin without further words. When Seth peered into the room only minutes later he found that she had dropped onto the lower bunk without bothering to even remove her vest or to pull a blanket from the upper berth before falling asleep.

He now lounged in the ship's comfortable pilot bench, his feet atop whatever debris had piled up on the console next to it. He ignored the usual jumbled confusion of the cabin; it rarely bothered him. On the days when it did he could be very thorough about cleaning his ship. Today was not such a day. He sat in the snug comfort of his home and sorted through the jumble within his mind.

He closed his eyes, remembering the conversation just a few days ago that had led him here. He had stopped over on Magra Torley with nothing more on his mind than feeling solid ground under his feet for a few days. Then a messenger arrived to change that plan

"I heard you're between jobs, Kada," a grating, high-pitched voice had roused Seth from the near doze he enjoyed that afternoon.

He had opened his eyes just enough to see a scrawny Human perched on the edge of his tub as if by invitation. "I'm on vacation, Zizzy, so you better piss off before I feel the need to drown someone." He closed his eyes again and tried to recapture the incredible sense of relaxation he had found here, immersed in biting hot water and fragrant steam.

"You Centauri have an exaggerated need for cleanliness," Zizzy said, apparently not afraid for his life.

"You should try it. What do you want?"

"It's what Pe Khoja wants that you should worry about."

Seth opened his eyes again. The rebel leader's name was not something spoken above a whisper around here. "What does he want?"

"Easy job, if you're up to it. There's a shipment leaving Pelion that needs to be stopped. Going outbound on a private freighter. Pe Khoja wants that shipment." He gestured vaguely. "A glass box about this big."

Seth looked around the bath house. He saw no one within earshot and the few other patrons were, as he had been, blissfully enjoying the quiet haven of water, clean tiles and well-worn wood. An appealing blonde hovered around the massage tables, looking like she might be up for a little private entertainment. "Why are you boring me with this, Zizzy?"

"The box is getting an Air Command escort out of rebel territory. Seven or eight. Plain clothes. Could get nasty if they don't want to give it up. Pe Khoja's not too concerned about their survival rate."

"What's in the box?"

"Water ash. 'Bout half and half pure."

Seth sat up in his tub and ran his hands through his hair to squeeze the water from it. "Why are they shipping water ash on a bloody cargo ship? Isn't that stuff poisonous?"

"As aerosol, extremely. You do not want to open that box. It's also hugely valuable. A bucket of that would keep a pharmaceutical concern going for a decade. But it's what else is in the box that has Pe Khoja all excited."

"What would that be?"

"I have no idea, but it's alive. Some anaerobic squid-thing from one of the Pelion moons. I'm not up on my xenos. Apparently they like water ash as long as it doesn't oxidize. Not too clear on that."

"What does Pe Khoja want with it?"

"Hey, I don't ask questions. I'm just getting his crew together. You want the job or not? Freighter is leaving Pelion in..." The Human paused to check a screen on his wrist. "Two days, our time. You'll make it if you hurry. What do you say? Want to play pirate?"

Seth stood up, not particularly worried about splashing the messenger when he turned on the overhead taps to rinse the soap from his body.

"Watch it!" Zizzy jumped away from the edge of the tub.

"Afraid to get clean?" Seth smiled at the blonde when she brought him a large bath sheet. The smile she returned definitely included an invitation. He stepped out of the tub and wrapped the sheet around his waist. "Let me see the guards."

Zizzy held up his wrist unit for Seth to study. "Pilots, skycops off Zera, side-loaded into this crap assignment for lack of other agents in the area."

"I'm a pilot," Seth reminded him. He scrolled the pictures over the screen to memorize the agents' faces. When Nova Whiteside appeared on the display he turned his surprised gasp into a cough. "Who else is going?"

"Gwain's crew, I'm guessing."

"Gwain's an idiot. He's got no grip on his people." Seth's thumb traced the edge of Nova's face. Even the greasy screen did not obscure the bright green eyes sparkling in a face sternly composed for the camera. He thought it a shame that her long mane of copper hair was pulled out of sight in the picture.

"That's why Pe Khoja wants *you* to take the box," Zizzy said.

Seth sighed dramatically and released the man's arm. "All right. Tell him I'm in. But he better be paying in large numbers if I have to handle that box. I like my lungs the way they are."

That had been just two days ago, Targon time. Seth's thoughts returned to the present and the untidy interior of his ship. Pe Khoja would not be pleased about the spilled tank. Other than the valuable substance in the box, of what significance was that creature? He considered sending a coded message to his contact on Targon to see what may be found there but then thought better of it. The less interaction with Air Command's headquarters, the better.

And what about Nova, now here on his ship? He left the cockpit to walk back into the cabin, stopping to retrieve the gun she had tossed onto the lounger. Perhaps it was best to keep the hardware out of her reach for a while. He smiled at the thought. If needed, Nova could probably fashion a weapon out of pillow.

She had been long out of his mind although the weeks they spent together those years ago were some of the most pleasurable in his memory. Capable, beautiful, possessing a mercurial temper, she had made each of those otherwise dreary days exciting and interesting. He could admit that, after Nova, he had never been able to look at a red-haired woman without a strange longing for what he had given up. Maybe she hadn't been out of his mind, after all.

THREE

"Do you know what this meeting here was about?"

"No, sir, I do not." The Human's brow furrowed as he pondered the question, posed amicably across the glass conference table by what was likely the most powerful of the Ten Elected Factors ruling Trans-Targon.

He looked over the debris left behind after the meeting. Cups and bowls, discarded notes and ignored reports, someone's forgotten respirator and, inexplicably, a pair of gloves. With temperatures soaring beyond endurance for most Humans and Centauri on this planet, why would anyone need gloves? He brought his attention back to the Factor. "I saw civilians leave. I'm guessing investors perhaps, considering where we are."

Factor Rellius, a Centauri who had actually spent a good part of his life in the far distant Centauri sector, rose to his feet and walked to the large windows overlooking Talan An, Feyd's capital city. Ancient architecture sprawled over the valley floor beyond the commercial blocks allocated to the Commonwealth, glaring in white-washed splendor under the relentless Feydan sun. In contrast, this citadel of climate-controlled comfort rose like a fortress above it all. "Indeed, investors," he said. "To put it more precisely, the sort of people who make life in Trans-Targon possible for us."

"Sir?"

"I am talking about trade, Drackon. What is the single most valuable commodity that comes to us from Centauri?"

Sam Drackon again glanced about the room, wondering why the Factor had chosen this day to lecture him. "Sir, if this is about the incident near Pelion—"

"Oh, just indulge me." The Factor busied himself with straightening an impeccable fold on his impeccable suit.

"Well, most of our buying power here comes from importing ordium from the Proxima system, I believe. It hasn't been found here in Trans-Targon."

"Indeed. And our job is to make sure that everyone here wants it. So now the stuff is worth several thousand times more here than it is on Centauri even after the cost of shipping which, I don't need to remind you, takes two years. And what does Centauri want in return?"

"Water ash," the Human said grudgingly. He loosened his uniform collar, feeling the star-shaped insignia as he did so.

Factor Rellius clapped his hands together in delight, just once, as if his favorite pupil had just given a correct answer. "Water ash. Exactly." He paused as if something just now occurred to him. "Or *Dous Tion*, if you want to get technical. One wonders who ever decided to call it water ash, considering that there's neither water nor fire were you'd find water ash."

Drackon shrugged, annoyed by Rellius' games. "It's a powder. It floats."

"Indeed. And now we have an entire planet just covered in it. Not a lake here and there, scattered all over the sector. But one single source with enough ash to supply Centauri for the next millennium. All we have to do is go to Naiya and scoop it up." He pondered the prospect for a moment. The light slanting into the room turned his violet eyes into flat, lifeless disks. "And here you are to tell me that the one thing that threatens the entire glorious enterprise is a squid in a box you failed to capture. Am I correct?"

"Yes, sir. The operation near Pelion did not turn out as

planned. Air Command has only limited movement in that region. My available resources for that type of covert operation, as you know, are utterly inadequate." He paused when Rellius' expression made clear that he had little concern for the means that would bring about the ends he sought. "I have a report with me," he said.

The Factor gestured vaguely and with extreme disinterest for him to go ahead. Drackon rose and walked to a screen at the head of the table. There were no technicians in this room, no agents, no guards, not even someone to display the presentation for these two men. The sort of meeting held by Factor Rellius and Colonel Drackon required no one else at the table. "Our analysis of the data sent from Pelion contains some valuable information." He activated the screen.

Rellius looked up to see a dimly lit corridor, possibly aboard a large ship or perhaps a remote outpost station, judging by the utilitarian design.

"This is the interior of the *Dyona*, owned by Pel-Aram, a shipping company out of Pelion. She was boarded just prior to entering the jumpsite toward Aikhor and Magra."

The Centauri nodded. Several people in protective clothing and full-face masks walked the hallway. Some were recording things, others waved sensors around. No one seemed to bother much about the corpses littering the floor.

"This recording was made only a few hours ago," the officer said. "There were no survivors aboard. Our team was able to download the records of the ship's internal surveillance system." He skipped to another segment. "Here is the event with the sample."

Rellius watched two men and a red-haired woman in some sort of cabin aboard the ship. His expression did not change when the pirate struck the woman but he frowned when the tank shattered on the cargo level. "I will suggest you review what sort of renegades you employ in the future, Colonel. A little competence goes a long way."

Drackon agreed absolutely but did not say so aloud. "Observe the next few minutes." He slowed the tape which now showed the incident from a different angle. The image brightened where his technicians had attempted to pick up additional details and zoom in on the subject. The creature slid from the broken tank and crawled onto the woman. Its limbs seemed too slippery for her to free herself. The recording slowed to a frame-by-frame display as one of the being's limbs wrapped around her neck. Whatever happened next was clearly painful and they watched her body convulse and stiffen. One of the pirates jabbed the creature to push it away from the Human. The video froze and zoomed in further. They were now able to make out a stinger or proboscis inserted into her neck, if only for a moment.

"This is not behavior previously observed among that species," Drackon explained. "They are called Myrids but little is known of them. Sentient and presumably intelligent but they do not inhabit the type of environment that would make interaction with any of our species easy or even necessary."

"You wouldn't be showing this to me if that woman was among the dead," the Factor said. He returned to the table and took his seat again.

"No, sir." The video skipped to another segment. A hallway again. This time they watched a black-haired man wearing a respirator, one of his hands around the woman's arm, the other holding a weapon. The woman was now also wearing a mask. The video froze and zoomed again.

"Who's that?"

"We have not been able to identify him in any of the video segments on which he appears. Pe Khoja moves his men frequently and we don't have records of them all. This one took the woman off the ship. Private cruiser."

"Centauri, obviously." Taller and longer-limbed than the Humans standing nearby, the Centauri was most easily identified by the mild glow of his eyes which *Dyona*'s cameras faithfully recorded. But his respirator hid his other features and he kept his face tipped toward the floor.

"Yes. He's avoiding the cameras on purpose. And he

knew or suspected that the air was bad even before coming aboard, or at least shortly after. Other passengers were removed from the ship but this Centauri left with just with that one woman."

"Who is she?" The woman appeared to be Human, possibly Feydan. Her long hair was deeply red, her skin very pale - an unusual combination on sun-baked Feyd. Without the long skirt from the earlier scene, he saw a fit, long-muscled body that set her apart from the rest of the rabble aboard the ship.

"One of ours, actually. Nova Whiteside. Air Command, First Lieutenant. Decent record. Decorated. She did a hard tour on Bellac Tau and so she is cooling off on a six month skycop stint over Zera, monitoring rebel activity near the jumpsite." Drackon let the video resume to show Nova and Seth rush toward the locks. "Both of them were able to leave the ship. From some of the segments, it appears that she did not go willingly."

"Where is the freighter now?" the Factor asked.

"We reported that, when the rebels tried to take it to Magra, they overloaded the intakes and caused a fatal chain reaction in the crossdrive. It happens. Some of those boats out there are poorly maintained."

"Good thinking. And the box?"

"There was nothing useful to be salvaged from the tank. The sample was tainted and mostly oxidized by the time our techs arrived."

"At least it's destroyed, even if I can't applaud the competence of your hired help, Colonel." The Factor tented his fingers and tapped them thoughtfully against his chin. "But at least now we know for certain that those troublesome Delphians are somewhere on Pelion. It's pure luck that we were even made aware of the shipment. If they hadn't asked for a secure transport, the damn box would be halfway to Naiya by now."

"Even if it had gotten out there, I assure you that the breach to Naiya itself is heavily guarded."

"By Shri-Lan rebels." Rellius looked like something disagreeable had left a terrible taste in his mouth. "Thugs and pirates."

Drackon nodded. In most parts of Trans-Targon, so-called rebels were little more than freedom fighters who chafed under the growing influence of the Commonwealth. They had dealt with these conflicts ever since the first fleet arrived from Centauri over three hundred years ago. A little sabotage, some angry speeches, or sporadic violent confrontations often required little more than negotiations, compensation, and the occasional military intervention to settle.

The rapidly growing Shri-Lan faction, however, had turned into a violent militia of worrying proportions over the past dozen years or so. They had weaponry, planes, hidden bases on many planets and even a few battleships financed through theft, drugs, smuggling, slavery and extortion. Their sabotage ranged to murder, kidnap and the destruction of entire towns on Union-friendly planets. Because of them, the Union's Air Command was expanding at a phenomenal pace, taking up vast resources better used for civilian and commercial ventures. Rellius found the entire situation tedious. Expensive and tedious.

"The sooner we get out of that deal, the better," he said. "Having to make a deal with rebels is giving me indigestion. But I don't suppose we have a better option at the moment. I want Naiya kept invisible until we can get a jumpsite charted and our claim to that planet secured. Who better to keep everyone out of that sub-sector than a horde of murdering thugs, eh?"

"Sir, I still believe it would be better if we could train up our own people to take on these covert operations. If we increased our resource of agents by just a hundred, even, we would not have to rely on rebels and pirates."

"Out of the question. I'll not have Union agents aware of our special projects. It's not a risk I'm willing to take. Use the rebels. They've served us well so far. Dispose of them when we no longer need them."

Colonel Drackon sighed. It was an old argument.

Rellius nodded as if Drackon had agreed with him. "How much longer will it take to stabilize the way to Naiya?"

"I'm afraid we're weeks away from properly charting that breach. The keyhole is dangerously unstable. We've lost one survey vessel already. I can't spare any more without someone noticing that they've been reassigned. My cartographers are doing what they can but we need a Level Three spanner or risk losing more. Until the jumpsite is established we can't start work on Naiya at all."

The Factor's already unhappy expression clouded even more. Invisible until mind and machine combined to delve into specific coordinates, a keyhole was little more than an unstable breach in normal space. It took a tremendous amount of energy and mental prowess to expand this breach and span the nothing within to reach the other side of the entangled equation. Without the efficiency of a charted jumpsite, Naiya's fabulous wealth would remain out of reach, only a few seconds away.

"And meanwhile those meddling beakers on Pelion are no doubt cooking up another batch of the catalyst at this moment."

"It may well be the last lab equipped to do so," Drackon said. "We've eliminated a few others. I think we can assume it'll take the Delphians a while before they can try again. We'll find them before then."

"Good. Even the thought that such a catalyst exists is giving me nightmares. I want it gone. And I don't want any remnants of it in the wrong hands." He tapped the display controls to move back to a still frame of Nova in the creature's desperate embrace. "This is the part that worries me, Colonel. We might be looking at the wrong hands."

The officer nodded. "We have considered it. Is it possible? Could the Myrid have transferred the catalyst to that woman?"

"It could have been reacting to the situation. A sting or

bite out of fear for its life. At this point we can't assume anything. I cannot stress enough how much the water ash resources on Naiya mean to all of us here. We will not lose control of it, we will not hand that planet to our competitors, and we will not let that catalyst reach its destination. Nothing else matters at this point."

"Understood, sir. We have started our investigation. If she's held by pirates she'll find a way to come in. She's proven her resourcefulness in the past. If she's in Shri-Lan hands we may have a more difficult time locating her, although they may try to ransom her."

The Factor shook his head. "I don't want her located. I don't want her to come in. For now we will report her lost with her team on the freighter. You will make sure the story turns out to be true. Then you will finally find the Delphians that started this whole nonsense and eliminate them, too. It's time we cleaned house. I want that catalyst wiped out of existence."

"Sir, the lieutenant is the daughter of Colonel Tegan Whiteside. There will be questions, investigations. She is not a common soldier."

The Factor turned. "*That* Whiteside?" He took a deep breath and released it as a drawn-out hiss as he considered this news. "All right, let's leave your people out of this. I'll assign one of my own staff to her. Let Pe Khoja know what you need once you locate her."

"Yes, sir," Drackon said, hiding his relief as best as he could. Taking out an Air Command officer was not an order he cared to issue. But in the unwritten, more clandestine policies guiding the Union, the Factors were allowed a team of private agents, proxies by any other name, who would carry out that order without question. Only the Ten Elected Factors, the absolute governors of the Commonwealth of United Planets, wielded the kind of power that would give them the authority to remove an Air Command officer without tribunal. These proxies, who did not officially exist on any Union roster, were the means to cut quickly and cleanly through the mire of politics, red tape and public opinion that would otherwise grind their government to a halt.

It was a good system, Drackon thought as he watched the Factor leave the room without farewell, as long as you weren't on the wrong end of the gun sight.

FOUR

"I don't suppose you have some clothes I could borrow?"

Seth looked up from his reader when Nova entered the main cabin. She had slept for so long that he, still worried about the effects of the water ash, had checked more than once to assure himself that she was still breathing. "Ah, it's awake. I was beginning to think I'd have to make breakfast myself."

"Well, don't expect me to." She perched bleary-eyed on the edge of the lounger. "I don't think I slept at all. Why is your ship so noisy?"

He looked around the silent cabin. The ventilation system made the only sounds, little more than a soft whirring noise from the overhead vents, along with the usual blips and squawks from the cockpit as he monitored nearby transmissions. The crossdrives had been powered down since he had set the *Dutchman* into a high orbit above Aikhor. Not even the music that usually accompanied his days aboard the ship was playing today.

"Take whatever you want in the cabin," he said. "Something there should fit you."

She nodded and rose again. "Neatness was never your greatest virtue," she mumbled, surveying the interior of the ship. "How do you find anything?"

"Did you want to express gratitude for my hospitality or just comment on my housekeeping?"

She waved his question aside and stepped into the tiny hygiene station near the ship's exit. The hot steam seemed to breathe some life into her tired limbs and she felt more or less awake by the time she returned to the crew cabin. There she pulled apart a few tangles of clothes and peered into Seth's storage, finding a long black shirt that fit quite nicely. She topped it with a vest made of intricately knotted leather strings that she suspected was worth a small fortune.

When she emerged again Seth handed her a strong cup of tea laced with a mild stimulant made of some sort of bean. She sipped the drink, sighing when she felt a soothing warmth move through her body. "I see you found my favorite shirt," Seth said. "It looks better on you, I think."

"Thank you. When are we landing?"

He raised an eyebrow. "In a hurry? We can go down any time. You should eat something first. The food there isn't any better than what I have on board, believe me."

"What is that place?"

"Aikhor? It's a dump. Frontier no-man's land but it's right in the middle of a few crucial jumpsites. We'll head to Magra in the morning. I have to tell you that the only female things that aren't native here are rebels or hookers." He inspected her with exaggerated appreciation. "Given your choice of attire, I see you're not a working girl."

She sneered at him. "I want a gun."

"Of course you do." He went into the ship's galley and rooted around a few bins to find a tray that looked like it hadn't been in there for too long. He inserted it into the heater. "I'm afraid we'll have to stay overnight. By the time we get down there we won't find a mechanic. I ripped two pogs when we left the freighter. That's going to take some time to replace."

There was a ledge by the galley with two tall stools and she came to perch on one of them. "I want to send a message," she said.

"Oh?"

"My father will have heard about the attack on the *Dyona*. He'll be worried. I'm sure my CO is, too. They probably think I'm dead or captive. I want to let them know I'm on my way back."

"You can send a packet from Aikhor. Not from this ship. I don't want it tagged. Besides, last time your father caught us holding hands he promised to transfer me to Chitta Moor to shuttle miners for the next three years. I remember that well. You might not want to tell him that you're aboard my ship."

"I think the report Archer sent was about more than just holding hands." She watched him peel the lid from the food tray he had heated for her. "So are you really a rebel?"

He made a sound somewhere between a laugh and a cough. "I thought I was a pirate."

"You're no pirate."

"If you thought I was a rebel you would have shot me yesterday. It's how you Air Command types deal with them. You don't ask questions and you don't have tea, first." He handed her the tray.

She inspected, with trepidation, the stringy bits of something floating in a gray mash. Nutritious, wholesome and not likely to offer anything remotely resembling flavor. "Let's just say I'm not sure you're *not* a rebel."

"I could do something rebellious, if you're looking for clarity."

"Why are you mocking me? When did you get so turned around? You used to be Union as much as I am."

He shrugged and picked up his teacup. "I've been on ground level for a while. That's where you see the results of the fire you sky jockeys lay down. It's not always the enemy that gives it up for you."

"I'm aware of that. I just got off Bellac Tau. That peace

came at a massive price, but it is peace now. Bellac is free of rebels."

"It's *not* free of rebels but if being owned by the Union now means peace then I suppose peace it is. The collateral damage doesn't bother you?"

"Whether it bothers me or not doesn't make the win any less important. And it's an alliance. We don't own planets." She pushed the tray away. "Sorry, that just looks too much like mud. I'll take my chances on Aikhor."

"Hey, want to fly the *Dutchman*?" he said suddenly.

Her frown dissipated at once. "Do you have to ask?"

She followed him into the cockpit where both took to the benches. In response, the ship's navigational systems shifted into ready mode, awaiting their orders.

"Not as automatic as the cruisers you've probably been flying. You might want to use the interface." Seth pointed at the headset hung above the co-pilot's chair. It would take just a few minutes for the ship to recognize the neural link module embedded in her temple and create a program for her.

"You have no faith," she said, impatient to get under way. "Watch and learn."

He rolled his eyes and engaged his own interface. "Just in case," he said. The lights on the control board came to life, confirming a connection between the ship's central processors and his brain via the implant at his temples. "Orbit break ready."

She studied the flight plan he had already laid in. Their destination was a town near one of Aikhor's many oceans and they'd approach from there. "Too easy," she said.

"Just remember the pogs," he said, his mind on the sensors. "And keep an eye on the weather. It's a stormy place. I'll compensate, if that's all right with you."

"Stop worrying. And if you think you've distracted me from my question, you are very much mistaken." She began their descent into Aikhor's atmosphere, feeling the plane shudder and balk at the rough treatment. Seth had been right; the entry required her full concentration. The *Dutchman*'s design made it a stallion among cart horses and just as temperamental. She laughed in defiance of the elements when they approached the planet and she leveled out into the promised turbulence.

Dense clouds hovered along the coast, obscuring much of the town although they saw lights here and there in the fog. Without any useful visibility, she finally relinquished control of the ship to Seth and watched while he brought the *Dutchman* into a vertical descent above an airfield using only his thoughts to direct the ship to its destination. His mental touch was deft; they felt the plane contact the tarmac with barely a wobble.

He opened his eyes to see her watching him. "Was I snoring?"

"Admit it. You were impressed by that entry."

He climbed out of the pilot bench and went into the cabin to pull a coat and a poncho out of a bin. "I was busy checking the weather. It's raining outside, mostly water. And it's cold. Atmospheric conditions are fine; we won't need any special gear. Gravity is a bit heavy."

"I noticed." She took the poncho from him and then held out her hand.

He pretended to consider. "Promise you won't shoot me?"

"No."

He sighed and moved past her to open another cabinet. She whistled in appreciation when she saw his arsenal of long guns and side arms. "Take your pick. Just make sure it's concealed. Their laws a little restrictive here."

She chose a projectile pistol in consideration of the weather and attached it to her belt under the poncho.

Outside the *Dutchman*, Seth consulted with a technician that had strolled out from the main building, apparently not bothered by the rain. Nova huddled under her cloak, listening to heavy drops fall onto her hood and thinking that, aboard a ship, even the dead emptiness of space was a lot more comfortable than the weather on most planets she had visited.

The rain tapered off even before they had reached the fog-swathed perimeter of the small airfield. These outskirts of the harbor town were little more than slums where few of the structures seemed built solidly enough to withstand the damp and wind.

Nova studied the pale-skinned and hairless natives with interest. Large oval heads topped barely clad, thin bodies. Most of them moved on both hands and feet that looked more or less alike. Nova and Seth hardly caused the raising of a single eyebrow, were such a thing available here. Off-worlders were not an uncommon sight on Aikhor.

Amused, Nova watched two children ride along on a parent's bent back. They were young; their eyes had not yet opened. "Twins and triplets are more common here than single births," Seth explained. "Infant mortality is pretty high."

The crowd of fleet-footed natives was heavily interspersed with foreigners and Nova, rarely with enough time or funds to indulge in travel, watched them all in wide-eyed amazement. She did not notice that someone had barred their way until she nearly bumped into him.

The being's skin was of a faded yellow but bristled with coarse gray hair. She gathered that it was speaking to her as it emitted a series of sighs and wheezes through some of its apertures. It wore no clothing and, by Nova's standards, it was quite obviously male. Unlike her and Seth, he was not part of the group of genetically and inexplicably related species found throughout Trans-Targon, usually referred to as Primes.

He raised a fibrous limb and wrapped two digits around her wrist.

"Hey!" She wrenched her hand from his grip.

Seth stepped closer to her. He gestured in a few halting movements. Nova tried to follow the incomprehensible body language as the creature answered. The exchange continued for a while until Seth gave a final wave and nudged her to continue walking.

Once at a safe distance, he reached into his coat to switch his gun back to its safety setting. "You're worth a lot of money here."

"What?"

"He wanted to buy you. Or rent you for a while. As a sort of decorative object, I think."

"So where does he keep his money?" Nova shuddered.

He laughed. "Over there is an inn of sorts. It's run by a couple of Centauri. It's not bad, considering where we are. Rent us some rooms, will you?" He handed her a wrapper with some currency. "Don't use your Union credit here, although they'll take it if they have to. I'll be along in a while and don't you worry about me running off to my rebel friends."

"Where are you going?" Nova said, immediately suspicious.

"Miss me already, honey?" He patted her rump.

"Stop that! Can't we sleep on the ship?"

"Too noisy with the repairs going on." He wandered away without further explanation, apparently expecting her to follow his instructions.

Ready to find some place that wasn't damp, Nova crossed the narrow street and entered the hostel. As nondescript as any colonial edifice on these remote worlds, it seemed to have been here for a while. She sniffed disapprovingly when she walked into the chilly reception hall. The smell of age and decay clung to this place like a wet blanket. Two elderly females were engaged in rolling up a large, knotted carpet, possibly the source of the mildew, its patterns indiscernible beneath a layer of mud. The crones gaped at Nova and then fell to whispering.

Belatedly, Nova rearranged her poncho to drape over her sidearm. She approached an obese Centauri by the desk, apparently asleep. His faded uniform bearing the inn's name was very clean in stark contrast to the moldy hall. "Good day," Nova said, assuming that this was still daytime. "Two rooms, please, the best you got, clean if possible."

The guardian of the lobby wheeled his chair closer to her. Although she wore Seth's clothes instead of a uniform, he took time to study her carefully. She was aware that the Union mainvoice she used was clipped and much abbreviated, a dialect used mainly by the military. Possibly, he was trying to decide if she was one of those meddlesome Union patrols sent into neutral territories to look for rebels. At length he shrugged; her origin was of no concern to him.

"We got rooms. Clean ones."

"I need to send a message. Tight band."

"Where to?"

"I asked for a tight band, didn't I?"

"We don't often get big secrets 'round here. Take your chances with what we've got."

Nova paid him for the rooms and followed his directions to the video booths in the rear of the lobby. There, she entered the delivery instructions, addressing her commander. Once complete, the recording would be sent by a relay through the jumpsite they had just used to the one near Zera and on from there to her base.

Someone rattled the handle to her booth, shouted something and moved on to the next. Nova leaned her back against the door.

The light beside the camera window came on. "Major," she began brightly. "I wanted to check in to let you know how much I appreciate the shore leave you granted. As you can see, I'm in good health even after the trip from Pelion. I'm sorry that we were not able to complete our assignment. I'll pick up a transport from Magra to Targon and await orders there. Please send a message to my father to let him know I'm fine. Whiteside out."

Nova's hand hovered over the command field to send the message packet to the relay. Should she advise them about Seth? She glanced up at the camera panel to consult her blurred reflection. What would she say? What had she seen?

He had hurt no one and he had saved her life. Should she implicate him from here, without evidence? No doubt they, by now, would have more intelligence about what had happened on the *Dyona* than she did.

She slapped the console to dispatch the message as she had recorded it and left the booth and then the inn without examining her decision. In the spirit of exploration, she wandered through the soggy streets until she found a shop that sold clothing to species like hers. Now using a trade language that had about as many different dialects as people using it, she dealt impatiently with the difficult currency, spending too much of Seth's money on a few drab and unadorned articles, apparently in fashion on this drab and unadorned planet. She was glad to return to the malodorous inn, away from the dreary streets.

Seth had been correct in his assessment of the local fare but she forced herself to eat a bowl of stew whose ingredients likely wouldn't have improved her appetite had she inquired about them. As far as she recalled, her immunity boosters were up to date. But she felt drained, affected by the high gravity dragging her arms and legs to the floor. Having nothing better to do, she made her way to the upper floor of the inn to find sleep in her room.

Harsh sounds woke her in utter darkness and, for several panicked seconds, Nova was unable to remember where she was and why she was sleeping in some type of sling. The room she had rented for Seth adjoined her own and she heard something crash to the floor in there, followed by a muffled curse. Then she heard the sound of a scuffle.

Her definition of 'clean' was not the same as the clerk's and she took care to slip into her boots directly below her hammock. She went to the other sling to search for the gun among her parcels.

In the hall, Nova sidled along the wall to the door of Seth's room. Feeling rather foolish, she stepped over another hotel guest who had elected to sleep in the hall. Looking closer, she saw that there were two of them.

Seth's door was ajar.

She peered into the room. "Seth? Is that you?" she whispered, her gun ready. "Seth!"

He was leaning against a small table that had once supported a lamp now wearily blinking on the floor where it had fallen. A very small female of Bellac origin was holding him up. Her skin was deeply red except for a network of purplish veins around her neck. The white hair was tipped with exuberant shades of pink and purple dyes. She wore only a brief kilt that did not hide a white tail; Nova could not tell if it was her own.

"It's all yours, darling," the Bellac warbled in an oddly inflecting accent. "I sure as rocks can't get any business out of that tonight."

Nova lowered her gun. "Get out."

"You're lucky I brought it back."

"Out!"

The girl's white-painted lips parted in a smile. Waving silvery nails at Nova, she stalked out with a saucy swish of her tail.

Seth dropped into his hammock. "I am not well at all."

Nova bent to pull his boots off. Like her own, they were caked with gray mud. "Is that what you do in your spare time? Getting drunk and picking up hookers?"

"So?"

"She wasn't even Human."

He snarled. "Neither am I."

She regarded him, amused. "You weren't really going to..."

"What if I was?"

She turned to leave.

"Nova." Seth waited until she turned back to him. "I wasn't going to. She followed me. I think she was planning to rob me or something."

She shrugged. "You don't have to explain your hobbies to me. You better get some sleep."

He held his hand out toward her. "Will you sleep with

me?"

"No!"

"I thought we were friends."

"Were we? I wanted to be your friend, long ago. You left without a word. I don't want to be your friend anymore."

"You don't mean that."

"Yeah, I do." She bent to the lamp on the floor and switched it off.

* * *

Seth met her in the inn's dining room in the morning. She looked up from the small screen attached to their table, ignoring the signs of his hangover. He was pale and there were dark smudges below his eyes. "I got some information about the attack on the *Dyona* from the tower on Pelion."

He sat down to squint at the screen. After a moment he gave up. "What does it say?"

"Apparently she self-destructed before the rebel could board. Isn't that creative? All aboard presumed dead. No word about our cargo, of course." She pushed a bowl over to him. "They've got real food here."

He looked into the dish without interest. "Smells like feet."

"You're missing out on some fine feet." She winked. "That was a pretty little thing you picked up last night."

"What thing?"

"Some genetic mix-up from Bellac. With a tail."

"Was *that* what that was?"

"Lucky for you I didn't let her have her way with you." She bit into a piece of fruit.

"How can you eat?" He averted his eyes. "Uh oh."

"What? Gonna puke?"

"If you're done with that we could go. Like now, maybe."

"What—"

"That Magra over there knows me. Get up, don't rush."

They pulled their capes around their shoulders and traded the cozy comfort of the eatery for Khom Arat's perpetually soggy streets. "What was that all about? Was that man a rebel?"

Seth looked over his shoulder. "Hmm, yeah. Shri-Lan. Not one of my favorites. He'd like to cut my... nose off."

"Lovely." She peered into the fog, seeing nothing but the dark shapes of the buildings closest to them. "Can we leave this pit now?"

He stopped to consult his data sleeve. "I suppose."

Nova's curiosity grew as Seth continued to check the time during their walk back to the airfield. A glance at his data sleeve showed that it was set to the standard timing of the ship and not to the rhythm of Aikhor's slow rotation. She soon saw the scuffed hull of Seth's much repaired and modified *Dutchman* through the haze seeping through the town.

"Damn," Seth said. "Listen, I forgot to do something. Can you get the ship ready for launch?"

"Where are you going now?"

"Over there," he said and pressed his hand against the *Dutchman*'s key plate. "Don't worry about it. I won't be long." He disappeared into the mist before she could object.

Nova boarded the *Dutchman*, annoyed by his secrecy and convinced that whatever he was up to was bound to be trouble. She called Khom Arat's traffic control and cleared their takeoff before completing pre-flight. It kept her occupied; Seth's ship was a quirky bit of machinery and things just didn't seem to be where they should.

An incoming message announced itself with a loud, persistent buzzing from the com system. Nova opened the line. "Sethran Kada residence."

"Nova!"

"Seth? Where are you? Why are you calling here?"

"Take the *Dutchman* up and try to get telemetry on me. I'm on the harbor side. There is some kind of shipyard out there, then a long road leading up the coast. You should be able to pick up my signal."

"I won't be able to see anything," she objected but tilted

her bench back and fastened the restraints.

"Maybe you should have set your interface the first time I suggested it. Hurry up now." His words seemed forced between ragged gasps for air. Was he injured? Running?

"What's going on?" Nova signaled her intent to launch and rose into the air as soon as she received final clearance. "I'm heading north now. I see the sea. Sort of. It's a lovely shade of gray."

"There is an open field ahead of me. You can land there to pick me up. Try to–" Nova heard a jumble of voices in the background, some shouting and then the sound of weapons.

"Seth!"

"You could hurry up a little, honey." More weapons fire.

"There is the road." Nova's hands flew over the navigational screens floating above her. "You should be able to see me now." He showed as a moving target near a steep row of contour lines on her grid. She nosed the *Dutchman* down and added real-vid to the display before her. Mist swirled below her, rarely clearing long enough for her to see the ground. "This is less than good," she informed him. "I can't see you."

She caught a glimpse of red in the gray mass below. Seth had discarded his jacket, not only making himself visible to her but also pointing out his position to his pursuers. Nova saw several shapes converging on Seth; the flash of their lasers lit the fog like lightning, diffusing ineffectively. A slow grin spread over Nova's face when she turned the *Dutchman* toward Seth's hunters. She let the plane crash-dive only to pull it up into a hovering mode at the last possible moment, forcing the men to dive for cover or risk getting caught in her wave. It tested her skill against Aikhor's unfamiliar gravity and her limited experience with his plane but Seth seemed to have faith in her abilities and kept running. She swooped back and repeated the maneuver to give him a chance to gain some distance. Using her guns to chase them off would have been easier but not half as much fun. At last, she spun the *Dutchman* and landed on the far side of the field.

"I love this ship!" She lowered the exit ramp and hurried to the door. Seth turned before he had cleared the pogs. "Come on, what are you waiting for?" His pursuers, recovered from the surprise of her aerial acrobatics, were now running toward the ship. A projectile glanced off the *Dutchman*'s hull with a high-pitched whine. She recognized the small device in Seth's hand as a remote control detonator.

"Listen." He punched a sequence of number symbols onto the unit. Seconds later a fog-muffled roar of thunder reached her ears. Any echo from it was immediately absorbed by the mist. "Let's go! The town will be closed off. Hurry!" He shoved her into the *Dutchman* and raised the gate.

"What was that?"

Seth jumped into the cockpit. "Sit down. I don't have time to explain." He barely balanced the ship's interior before he used the emergency thrusters to gain additional velocity. Nova gritted her teeth. It was a clumsy, dangerous maneuver and she doubted that even Seth would dare execute it on any of the Union's strictly ruled airfields. She waited for the *Dutchman* to disintegrate into its components on the way out of Aikhor's atmosphere.

The ship quieted. She opened her eyes. A cup floated past her, spilling its contents in glossy beads as it turned. A paper map wrapped itself gently around her head. She unbuckled herself from her chair and floated back to the lounge to catch some of the weapons that Seth hadn't put away. At least he had minded the safety switches.

"If this place wasn't such a mess your life would be a whole lot easier." She groped for a boot.

He shifted the *Dutchman*'s power to spin up the gravity. Nova and the countless floating objects settled onto the floor of the cabin. "Pretty smooth, eh?" He adjusted their course and came up from the cockpit. With gravity once more restored, the cabin was twice the cluttered disorder than usual. Sighing, he began to sort through the heaps of clothes and tools on the floor. "That was some fancy flying there,

Nova. Your Hunter class tag is well deserved."

"I think you'd better explain what the hell you blew up down there."

"Just a place I didn't like. This weather ruined the detonator I wanted to use. I'll have to remember that in the future."

"A place you didn't like?" she said in astonishment. "Have you forgotten who I am? I am a Union officer, dammit. A cop! You can't just do that right under my nose. How dare you?"

He laughed. "I'm already under arrest so I thought one more fiendish act wouldn't matter. Although I'll point out once again that this isn't a Union planet, Officer." His eyes shone brightly as he chuckled to himself and continued to rearrange his cabin. Nova's ripe selection of curses seemed to roll off his back like water.

"You have a foul mouth for such a pretty woman," he said finally. "Comes from hanging out with pilots for so long. If you're done with that, I can explain."

"I know what I need to know about you. I need your help right now but that doesn't mean I approve of you. You've caused a lot of harm to a lot of people. Don't make me part of that, you pirate."

"There are reasons."

"Like what? Because Tharron pays so well for your services? If anyone had told me six years ago that you'd become a traitor I would have laughed."

Seth's expression hardened and his eyes gleamed dangerously in a deep violet when he turned to her. "That place I blew up down there was one of Tharron's labs. I've been looking for it for months and being your personal chauffeur wasn't going to cause me any more delays. In case you don't know, he owns a little Human doctor called Comori whose favorite pastime is to tinker with viruses and drugs and all types of nasty bugs. The kind Tharron likes to throw at Union settlements now and again. I thought I'd try to stop him for a while."

Nova bent to pick up a tangle of clothes. She did not look at him. "Why?"

"Because I don't like the Shri-Lan, either, and I like their boss even less."

She carried the bundle toward the cargo door. "And yet you work for him." She released the door and then opened one of the storage bays.

"Uh, Nova, wait—"

"What the hell is all this?"

He hurried into the cargo hold to find her leaning against a spring-loaded door to keep it from shutting.

The small storage chamber was stacked to the ceiling with long guns bundled carelessly in strips of cloth. Crates of what looked like thousands of rounds of projectile ammunition and rail gun power packs were secured to the floor. Some of the weapons were completely unfamiliar to Nova but at this point she had no thought for expanding her knowledge of firearms. She pried the lid off a plastic case embossed with Centauri ciphers. "Seth!"

The box contained dozens of sealed glass vials. She held one to the light. "You are gun running!" she accused. "Don't tell me this is your personal arsenal. That rail hasn't even been released yet. And this thing! We're into germ warfare now? Chemical? Drugs maybe? Not enough money in green stuff?"

He took the vial from her to replace it carefully in its padded compartment.

"Well?"

"I stole it on Aikhor. Before I went out to the lab. It was a lucky find, nothing more." He pulled her away from the door to let it shut again and returned to the main cabin. "People shouldn't leave things lying around unguarded."

"Stole it? That is Union issue."

He returned to the task of tidying the cabin. "Most rebel arsenal is Union issue."

"You stole this from rebels?"

"From people selling to rebels."

"Is that what you were doing half the night? Getting drunk and loading contraband?"

"Well, yes. Mostly. Don't forget the part about the hookers and blowing things up."

"You don't care what I think of you, do you?" she snapped angrily. "I don't understand you at all."

He frowned. "Understand me? I thought you knew me so well. Between us, I'm not the one who needs to be understood." He stood very close to her now, searching her face as if looking for someone he once knew. "What's happened to you? There isn't a soft spot left on you. You used to have a sense of humor. Where did that go? Don't expect me to stand in line with your squad pals. You of all people know me better than that."

"You left a long time ago. Things change. People change. Even if you haven't."

"I don't believe that," he said more softly. "You're in there somewhere, Red." He lifted his hand as if to touch her face but then placed it on her shoulder instead. "What did they do to you? Does this come from living in barracks for too long, marching up and down in front of Air Command brass for a few years? What happened to you on Bellac?"

Nova regarded him silently, aware of his hand, as deeply affected by his presence as she had been so many years ago. She could feel the warmth of his spirit as clearly as she could feel the warmth of his body only a handspan from her own.

She pulled away and forced a perky note into her voice. "Nothing happened on Bellac. I don't like rebels and I don't like smugglers. I'm a Union soldier and you'd better remember that. It's all there is." She dropped onto the lounger. "I'm too tired to argue with you. You're a better arguer than I am, anyway."

"Tired? You just got up a couple of hours ago."

"All that gravity, I guess. Or the weather down there."

"You look awfully pale. Do you hurt anywhere?"

She shook her head. "Just the sting I got on the freighter."

"Sting?"

She pointed at her neck. "Sting. Bite. Whatever it was that the thing in the box did to me."

He stared at her, stunned. "And you didn't think to mention that earlier?"

She frowned. "What did you think it was?"

"It looks like someone took a stunner to you, nothing more." He crouched beside the lounger and pulled the bandage from her skin to peer at it closely. "Yes, I can see the hole now. I thought it was a blister or something that had broken. What were you thinking? That thing lived in a water ash soup. Didn't you think it might be poisonous, too?"

"Not much I can do about it way out here, can I? I really don't love the idea of finding some clinic run by rebels. I'll be fine till I get to the base on Magra." She stood up, but too quickly. He caught her when she swayed on her feet as a wave of dizziness robbed her of her balance. He lowered her back down onto the bed.

"I'll set course for Targon," he said. "They've got the best exobiology labs in the sector."

"Targon? You know if you take me to the base I'll have to make a report on you, if they haven't identified you already. Those guns back there won't help your case."

"Ah, so that hole in your neck is an elaborate scheme to bring me to justice. Very clever, Lieutenant."

"I'm serious, Seth."

He shrugged. "I can't think of any way to get you there faster. We'll lose days if we go to Magra first to find a transport for you."

She looked up at him, blinking tiredly. "You'd do that? Go into Targon? For me?"

"Let's try some air. I don't know if it's such a great idea for you to sleep so much." He went into the cargo hold and returned with a small oxygen bottle.

She let him fasten a mask over her mouth and nose and then curled up in a corner of the lounger. "Just a little nap," she said. "Wake me for the jump."

FIVE

Nova was glad when the orange ball that was Targon appeared on their screens. This sponge-like planet, riddled with subterranean, water-filled cave systems, served as the military hub of Trans-Targon and the largest base in the sector. There was no reason to settle on the bland, inhospitable surface; those who needed to live nearby chose Odar, a not-too distant moon. Targon's close proximity to some of the most vital charted jumpsites made it a strategically well-placed headquarters; the absence of civilian targets made it an easily defended one.

Like many Air Command bases, it was drab and utilitarian but it also offered an academy and flight school where personnel attended lectures and upgraded their skills. Many also came to enjoy a play or perhaps a new artist or to meet friends stationed in other parts of Trans-Targon.

Nova had visited here once or twice before but never for long. It had always seemed to her like the most exciting place in the entire sector. She hoped to be stationed here someday. Today, however, she wanted only to see and be seen by the doctors of the base's well-equipped hospital. It had taken three days to make the journey from Aikhor to Targon through two jumpsites and endless hours of travel between the gates.

The additional oxygen had returned strength and energy to her and, although the debilitating fatigue remained, she was awake enough to join Seth at the helm or laze about the cabin while the autopilot did its job. They spent the time talking of nothing that lay ahead and certainly nothing that lay behind them, carefully skirting the issue of rebels and his part in her misfortunes. She was reminded again of the time they had spent just like this, when he would share with her his thoughts about the worlds and their inhabitants that held endless fascination for him. Information that was, to her, just figures and facts on a page came alive for him through stories and histories and what appeared to be real people and not just names on a screen.

Of course, back then they would spend these hours between long bouts of lovemaking, sprawled entwined in some hideaway until it was time to get back into uniform and into their planes. Now she did not dare to touch him even incidentally - his presence across the cabin was beginning to chafe her in ways both pleasant and entirely unwelcome.

"You better clear us," Seth said as they approached UCB Targon. "I don't think they'll let me land."

"Should security be anything but tight here?" she replied. "They know this ship, I'm sure. By now it'll be identified and traced to you. You better come up with a few explanations."

Seth nodded, looking at ease with the situation. She wondered if anything ever really worried him.

She contacted the base to request permission to land. Understandably, Targon's reply was delayed while somebody checked with someone to get permission from somebody else. She knew that the matter of clearance would be shuffled about until someone or somebody kicked it upstairs to the base commander.

Eventually, she was given landing instructions. Nova was surprised to hear that they were to move the *Dutchman* directly into the underground hangars instead of the public aboveground airfield.

"You want to shackle my hands and feet or something?" Seth said when they prepared to drop the cargo bay gate.

She looked up at him, suddenly unsure. Now that they were here, she no longer wanted to see him arrested, perhaps hurt, surely incarcerated for some time if her charges against him could be proven. "Seth..." she began.

He looked amused. "Don't worry, Red. I wouldn't be here if I didn't want to be."

Before she could reply the door fell open and they were surrounded by a cluster of white-clad base personnel. They pushed their way into the cramped cargo area and manhandled Nova onto a stretcher.

"Hey! It's only—"

"Please allow us, Lieutenant," one of the medics whispered. "By order of Colonel Carras." He leaned forward to let her see the identification tab on his collar beneath the hospital garb.

Mystified, Nova reclined on the stretcher and allowed herself to be covered up to her chin. She closed her eyes and was whisked out of the hangar and toward the base hospital.

Seth had watched it all with amazement. What was the colonel up to?

"Sethran Kada," a sharp voice rang out.

Still musing, Seth turned to see a half dozen guns pointed at him.

"Step away from the ship."

Seth obeyed, raising his hands slightly. He was searched roughly and thoroughly. "Carras' orders, right?"

"Search the ship," the guard barked and Seth was led away, out of the hangar.

A five-man security team ushered him along UCB Targon's maze of hallways. As they moved deeper underground, the slick, impressive design of the upper levels gave way to meaner, more utilitarian accommodations. There seemed to be no need for stylish wall treatments here and the installation's superstructure, at times even the cave walls, were exposed. They used a cage-like elevator and then a trolley to reach a sector which Seth had had occasion to view before today.

"Kada!" he was greeted once they had arrived at the nearly deserted cellblock. The walls here had been smoothed with some pale blue foam that was flaking off in places but at least the place seemed less like an underground bunker than the passages they had just traveled.

Seth smiled. "Spenser, my favorite turnkey. How's the hemorrhoids? Business good?"

The Human sneered. "Not as good as yours." He perused a monitor in front of him. "A hatch full of guns, I see. Arrested for piracy, it says. Don't look too good to me, son."

Seth shrugged. "Got my old room for me?"

"Sure. All I've got's a couple of discipline cases here. Another body or so'll keep the place from echoing. Maybe you'll stay a while this time." Spenser heaved himself onto his feet and led the way along a corridor to an empty cell. Once there, he gestured Seth inside with a grand flourish. "Just like you left it. Better rest up. You know how excited the boys can get when they think they're interrogating a real criminal. They're especially fond of rebels."

"Yeah. I remember. You got any food here?"

Spenser glanced at the guards behind him, then back at Seth. The question regarding food was a signal of the highest priority. DO NOT INTERFERE, it meant. Seth did not need Spenser's help to escape or to contact spies; he had reason to be on Targon.

"Wait yer turn," he said. "I'll be bringing my Points board, if you think you can beat me."

"With my hands tied." Seth raised his bound wrists. "Not that I've got a choice."

Spenser tapped his finger print a few times to a sensor on Seth's restraints to release his hands. "Just so you'll be forever grateful."

Seth stretched out on the cell's narrow bunk and watched the translucent door slide into place. Then he waited. Sooner or later Carras, Targon's military operations lead, would send someone to demand a few answers. He wondered what he would tell them.

He dozed uncomfortably. Mild claustrophobia nagged him relentlessly although he was well accustomed to the confines of his ship. A small enclosure never bothered him as long as he was able to steer it where he wanted to go. This stationary trap was something entirely different. He sat up again, feeling the walls close in. He hoped that the *Dutchman* had not been searched too thoroughly. It wasn't necessary for them to see everything his ship had to offer.

He was kept waiting for hours before voices near the guard station traveled down the echoing cellblock hallway. Footsteps, some of them the brisk pace of well-trained soldiers, approached and Seth came to his feet to await whatever was heading his way. His last visit here had cost him a tooth and he was uneager to repeat the experience.

Colonel Carras appeared on the other side of the door, accompanied by two guards and the jailer. The elder Centauri regarded his prisoner wordlessly before nodding to Spenser whose handprint opened the door. Carras stepped inside the cell. One of the guards handed him a box. "Leave us," he said to them.

The stone-faced soldiers complied. Seth threw a flirtatious glance at one of them and winked. She appeared not to have noticed.

Alone, Carras and Seth regarded each other warily.

"Long time, Colonel," Seth said.

Carras sat down on the other bench in the cell and tossed the box to Seth. "It has been. Can't say I'm happy to see you here."

Seth shrugged. "Nice of you to visit me down here personally, then." He sifted through the box containing his confiscated effects. He returned his gun to a holster beneath his jacket, another into the shaft of his boot and then pulled his data sleeve over his arm where it belonged. A quick check showed that it had not been accessed. A hefty amount of

Commonwealth currency and an electronic lock pick went into his pocket.

"Was feeling naked without this." He tapped the *Dutchman*'s control unit. "I brought you a present from Aikhor. You like it?"

"The guns? A present? I'd imagine that under other circumstances you would have looked for a buyer for them."

"Only among your people, of course."

"Of course," Carras said. "I have to say you're doing well for yourself. I couldn't help but admire your ship."

Seth smiled. "Not an Eagle, but she's got a lot of guts."

"Not exactly government issue. Tharron pays that well?"

"I have a few side ventures."

"What brought you to the *Dyona*?"

"Distress signal. I was in the neighborhood."

"And the guns?"

"Stole them. On Aikhor."

"From?"

"You know I'm not going to tell you that, Colonel."

"Why was Lieutenant Whiteside with you?"

"Seems like a nice girl."

"That nice girl is an Air Command officer whose so-far excellent future prospects aren't improved by your presence. Show a little respect."

Seth grinned. "I didn't touch her, I swear."

Carras looked half amused and half exasperated. "I have no doubt in my mind that Lieutenant Whiteside has more sense than to let that happen." He stood up. "Get off my planet, Kada. I want you gone by tomorrow."

* * *

Elsewhere on the base, Nova sat moodily on her bed by the window, legs folded under her, and looked out over Targon's barren landscape. Her eyes followed the flight paths of the planes above the base with longing. Passenger shuttles, cruisers, small freighter, even one or two of the powerful Eagles kept the landing bays humming. She counted the sleek Kite class fighter planes as they came from patrols and exercises and mentally waved after the departing ones. If only she could get out of this place and back into her own Kite where she belonged!

But here she was, stuck in this unnervingly silent hospital where, for some inexplicable reason, everything was white. Walls, floor, furniture, bedding, even the cozy two-piece lounging suit she had been given - everything white! She wondered if she should run up and down the hallway outside to see if she could at least get her paper slippers dirty. Then again, she thought, dirt was likely not allowed in the hospital, either, for lack of being white.

A nurse in whites entered her room with the sort of smile that was a requisite for working among the soon-to-be dead of squid bite. "We're about done with today's tests," he said brightly. "I'm sure that's good news. How do you feel?"

"Top shape for someone who's had a nanobot or two crawl through her veins," Nova said. "In fact, I think I'll go down to the mess hall for dinner."

"Not so fast," he said, his smile unwavering. "Doctors are on their way. I don't think you're going anywhere for a while." He poked around some of the monitors surrounding her bed. "Nice try, though."

She shrugged.

He turned when the door to the hall opened and then snapped to attention when two uniforms enter the room along with her team of doctors. Nova moved to get up, stopping only when the nurse held his hand out to keep her seated.

"I'm fine, really," she protested but he shook his head.

"Lieutenant Whiteside," Doctor Darshan greeted her, but his eyes were on her monitoring screens. "We're pleased you're feeling better. You'll be staying that way a while longer."

"So I'm not in any danger?" She directed a puzzled glance at the colonel and the major, both Centauri, who had accompanied the doctors. What had brought those two to her room?

"Well, no and yes," the doctor said. "You were definitely infected by something when that creature stung you. An agent was introduced into your bloodstream."

"What sort of agent?" Nova touched the small bandage on her neck.

"We're not sure, quite honestly. It binds with your hemoglobin, which is why you were, essentially, being suffocated. We attempted several transfusions but the substance is being replaced as fast as we can remove it."

She raised both eyebrows. "A parasite?"

"Hmm, nothing that lively. The substance becomes inert as soon as it leaves your blood and comes in contact with air. Its components are not complex but we don't understand how it lives, or even why. It is not a natural product of the creature that infected you."

"We suspect that the Myrid was a carrier," the colonel interjected. His voice had the pleasant drawl common among his people and, like all Centauri, he had a thick shock of black hair and violet eyes. But unlike his tall and slender kinsmen he was portly and his heavy jowls and chins resembled those of a Human. "It was used to move, perhaps smuggle, this material from Pelion to its destination. We suppose it requires a living host to remain viable."

"So that means that the xeno, this Myrid, did this on purpose? It wanted to preserve this... whatever it is?"

"Myrids are intelligent sentients, even if we cannot interact with them on any meaningful level. It likely realized that it was dying when the tank broke."

"So how are you going to get this out of me?"

"We are working on a solution, I assure you," Darshan said. "We will need some time. We have requested additional experts from Feyd and Delphi. Meanwhile, we can keep your blood stable to prevent further trouble with your oxygen exchange. I've ordered a supply of boosters from the dispensary that you can administer yourself." He placed a packet of single-dose ampoules on the tray by her bed. "Are you familiar with these?"

She nodded. A short needle would be affixed to the capsule to deliver the drug directly into a vein. "Yes, we used them on Bellac."

"One of those once a day and you're fine. We will run more tests in the morning but I'll try to get you back into civvies as an outpatient. How does that sound?"

"Frankly, I'd rather be back in uniform, Doctor." She nodded toward the window. "And my plane."

He smiled indulgently. "Yes, soon, I'm sure. The good news is that this agent in your blood seems to have rendered you immune to the poisonous effects of water ash."

"Well, now we can all celebrate," she grumbled.

"Doctors, please give us a few moments," the colonel said. His gesture included the nurse.

The officers waited while the medics filed out of the room before the colonel pulled a chair from the wall and sat down. "Lieutenant, I am, as you probably know, Colonel Tal Carras, commander of UCB Targon, and this is Major Bak. You seem to have had quite an adventure."

"I'm not sure about that, sir. It feels more like a bit of a disaster."

"We know what happened on the *Dyona*," he said. "The videos from all decks were transmitted with the distress signal. But the sound files are inconclusive. What do you know about this transport?"

She lifted her shoulders as she thought about his question and then dropped them again. "Not a lot, sir. We were sent from Zera to guard a Delphian leaving Pelion for Magra with that alien. Some scientific expedition going I guess. We were betting that it was something about to go extinct and was being relocated or a breeder or something, seeing how Delphians were involved. You don't see them traveling out there unless they're working on something like that. He didn't say much to us on the way out."

"Who shipped the box?"

"A regular freight company on Pelion arranged for the

trip and the security detail. We picked the box and the Delphian up ourselves rather than have him sent up to the *Dyona*. Lieutenants McLaine and Be'al went into the building. I stayed in the shuttle. We kept it under guard until the pirates boarded us. Things got out of hand quickly after that. I'm sorry, sir."

"Yes, we saw the video. The pirates opened fire after Captain Harlow refused to allow them entry into one of the cabins. Unfortunately, the *Dyona* was subsequently destroyed."

She sighed. "All this over a shipment of water ash? People were already dying by the time we escaped. Did you intercept any of the pirates? They took some passengers and crew off the ship before the air went bad."

"I'm afraid not," Carras said. "What was Sethran Kada's involvement?"

She glanced from him to the other officer before answering. "He arrived later, I think. I have... met him previously and he decided to take me off the ship. There was no time to save anyone else."

"You know him?"

She returned his questing gaze without wavering, not doubting that the Colonel already knew every turn her Air Command career had taken to get her to this moment. "Yes, sir. We trained together."

Carras nodded, apparently satisfied with her answer. "What was the intended destination of the tank?"

"I don't know, sir. We were to leave it with the Delphian on Magra Alaric. They just wanted safe passage out of rebel territory."

"Who approved the escort?"

"As I understand it, sir, the request was made directly to my CO according to our agreements with Pelion's governors. She's supplied security for transports on other occasions, although usually for passengers."

The colonel tapped his fingers on the armrest of his chair as he considered this. "You are temporarily relieved of duty,

Lieutenant. But you are staying on Targon until we have discovered a way to deal with that organism."

"I'm guessing that there is no intention of removing this thing from my blood until you've figured out what it is. Am I right?"

"Very astute. We have classified the entire incident. I've taken this case and you will answer any further questions only to me. You are to have contact with no one other than hospital staff. No further communications from you to anyone else about this."

"Yes, sir," she said, not inclined to question command decisions. "Colonel, about Sethran Kada... I would not be here if not for him. I did not see him harm anyone aboard the *Dyona*. He may be a common pirate but—"

"I assure you he is not a common pirate," Carras said. "He's been released from custody."

This time, Nova could not help but voice her surprise. "What? Why?"

"He's a civilian. We have no evidence of anything but that he helped you escape the *Dyona*. And you confirmed that. The guns in his possession were not contraband that we were able to trace." He stood up.

"Did he... did he leave?"

"His ship is still on Targon." He paused before opening the door. "You may want to reconsider any future connection with that man. He is at the very least a rebel sympathizer. Your record so far is flawless. Associations have a way of finding their way into your files."

"Yes, sir."

"Rest now, Lieutenant. We will return later to continue the debrief. I'm under orders by the good doctor to keep this interview short."

She smiled at him, feeling at ease with the Centauri. "Thank you, sir."

* * *

Nova awoke hours later when a spill of light fell into the

room. She blinked tiredly, watching a medic enter and increase the illumination just enough to see by. He stopped to peer at her for a moment before moving closer, to the side of her bed. She breathed evenly and slowly, her lids barely open. Something about his furtive movements seemed beyond the care someone would take around a sleeping patient.

The man froze when she shifted and waited for her to change positions in her sleep, perhaps unaware that she had pulled her blanket away from her legs. He reached into a pocket and withdrew something that he then placed onto her tray. When he turned to listen for a sudden sound in the hallway she saw the outline of a gun beneath his hospital whites. An adrenaline rush surged through Nova's veins to banish any remnants of fatigue from her system.

He did not draw the gun but instead took her wrist to turn her arm, his touch gentle and steady. When he twisted to reach for the object he had placed on the tray, Nova exploded from her bed to hook one knee around his neck, using her other foot to launch herself forward and throw him off balance. He stumbled and pulled her along when he crashed to the ground. It was an inelegant maneuver that relied mainly on surprise and was hindered by her disadvantaged position, but she managed to pin him face-down, his arms twisted painfully behind his back. She grasped his hair and slammed his head onto the floor, stunning him, before reaching up to snatch the item he had placed onto her tray. It was an ampoule similar to those Doctor Darshan had left with her.

"Time for my meds?" she asked.

He turned his head but when he tried to shake her off she leaned forward to twist his arm even further. Something popped. He groaned in pain but did not call out for help. Blood pooled under his face from a broken nose.

"Who sent you?" she said.

"Fuck you."

"You're not my type." She placed the needle-tipped vial

against his neck. "Who sent you?"

"You don't have the balls."

She stabbed the needle deep into his neck.

He squealed, not quite loud enough to alert nearby hospital staff. "Stop! Don't!"

"That's in your jugular now. I've had practice with these things, believe me. All I have to do now is give it a good squeeze. I suggest you hold still."

He made a small and unclear sound.

"I didn't quite get that. Who did you say sent you?"

"Pe Khoja," he said, sounding resigned and probably angry at having been taken down by her. "Some Caspian named Pe Khoja, out of Magra."

"Why?"

"I don't know. Take that thing out of my neck!"

Nova was running out of time. She felt the body beneath hers tense as he overcame the pain of his broken nose and assessed her hold on him. There were only moments before she would have to shout for help. "Who else on this base is working with him?"

"Not telling you anything, bitch. Go ahead, start yelling. I'm not alone here but you are. No one will come for you. The colonel made sure of that."

"Colonel?"

He lunged desperately away from the hand that held the deadly capsule to his neck and tried to push her away. Nova increased her now one-handed leverage on his arm but when he twisted to slide from under her the capsule between her fingers compressed. The liquid in the ampoule surged into his vein and she held him down while he convulsed beneath her for the longest twenty seconds of her life and the last of his.

Nova expelled something between a gasp and a sob as she rolled away from him. She stared at the ceiling, breathing heavily, desperate to calm her thoughts. What had brought this rebel here? Who was this Caspian, this Pe Khoja, if that information was true? What had he meant when he mentioned the colonel? There were thousands of people on this base and most certainly there were rebels among them. Were they operating at command level right here on Targon, the most vital military installation in the entire sector?

"Keep moving," she whispered to herself and struggled to her feet, counting her priorities. Get out of this place, regroup, if only with herself, find safety, think. She went to the door and peered into the hallway. No guards, no one in uniform, just the occasional medic and a few patients. And no way to tell friend from foe.

She looked down at herself. Her clothes had been taken away and all she had where these pajamas or whatever it was that they issued in this place. Blood from the assassin's nose stained one of the sleeves and more was smeared across her chest.

Nova bent over the dead rebel on the floor and tugged on his smock. When she rolled him over to remove it she also took his gun and felt instantly safer. His lab coat hid the gun and the blood on her clothes. Before heading for the door, she snatched her medication packet from the tray by her bed.

She slipped into the hallway and joined the other patients walking there, even at this late hour. Strolling among the insomniacs without hurry, she scanned the hallways for exit signs. One appeared overhead and she followed its suggestion to turn into another corridor. Medical staff and a few patients stood near a bank of elevators just ahead, waiting for their ride. Two uniformed and armed soldiers watched them closely, perhaps hoping for some malfeasance to liven up the late hours of their shift.

Nova retraced a few steps and used the key tab on the rebel's smock to open the door to a laundry supply closet. "Hate elevators, anyway," she grumbled and opened the hatch to the laundry chute. As she hoped, the shaft was outfitted with deep indents along the way to facilitate maintenance. It took just a few seconds for her to heave herself across the lip and begin the climb downward. She descended as fast as she could, not looking down, not wondering how many floors existed below the base hospital. Twice she had to flatten herself against the slick wall of the chute to avoid being swept along by bundles of bedding and towels. She stopped to remove her hospital slippers to find better purchase on the plastic footholds. She was not in the top physical shape she had been only days ago and she felt herself growing weaker with each floor she passed.

At last, light and cooler air reached her and she saw a mountain of laundry piled on the floor below. She gripped a metal rail at the bottom of the shaft and twisted to peer into the service hall. Seeing no one, she let herself drop, blessing the pile of unvarying whiteness that so closely matched her clothing.

After a moment's rest she rolled from the heap and stole along a system of conveyors, ducking behind bins when a worker or two strolled by. The laundry system was fully automated and few hands were required to keep things organized. It took an eternity before Nova found what she was looking for: a row of bins on tracks containing clean flight suits, helmet-pads, sub-gloves, and pressure suit liners along with the standard gray shirts and shorts worn by the pilots living in the barracks on the lower floors. She missed two of the carts that were abruptly put in motion and leaped into a third.

The containers whipped along on their tracks, jolting Nova at every turn and every sudden stop. She pulled a few bundles up between her and the sides of the bin to cushion the worst of the blows but the ride soon had her feeling queasy and disoriented. She managed to dig her way down to a flight suit of approximately her size and slipped into it. At last the cart slammed to a stop without due consideration of her already bruised shoulders, forcing a pained grunt from her.

She peered over the edge of the bin and, seeing no one here, vaulted out of it and across the rails before someone came to unload the cart.

"Now where the hell are you, Whiteside?" she murmured

and looked around. A nearby sign on a double-door showed that she was on the third level. She had no idea what the third level was for but, considering the flight suit delivery, assumed it to be flight decks. The base was built into the almost vertical side of an escarpment and the bays had been carved out of existing tunnel entrances leading deep below the surface. She pushed through the door and slipped into the hall beyond.

This level stood in sharp contrast to the antiseptic environment she had left above. The walls, bare and cracked in places, dripped unpleasantly. A cold draft met her, hopefully from open bay doors near the parking garages for the planes. She headed into the draft, shivering as she moved along the deserted corridors. Surely, Seth could be found near the *Dutchman*.

Eventually, her instinct and a few less-than informative signs led her to the hangars. She hurried along the perimeter of a vast parking garage, moving behind vehicles and supply crates when possible. She saw a few technicians working on a shuttle in the distance and a group of pilots walking toward one of the rear hallways.

There were no fighter planes on this level and the space was allocated to service cruisers, shuttles and private planes. Among them stood the *Dutchman*, recognizable by its low-slung cockpit tucked forward of the crossdrive assembly. Nova approached it and pressed her hand to the key plate by the entrance. She was not authorized to access this ship and so an alarm would sound inside. Nothing happened. She tried again, wondering if he was asleep. The attempt to enter the ship would also have sent an alert to his data sleeve.

Voices reached her ears from the glass-walled passage leading away from the hall. It was the boisterous sound of bored pilots amusing themselves with what little recreation was available down here. It reminded her of her own squad who would be doing the very same thing between shifts on her base on Zera. Then again, they had lost six of their number just days ago and she doubted that there was much laughing now. Seven, if her survival was also classified.

She moved toward the voices and soon entered a brightly-lit commons room where a half dozen pilots lounged around a game board, sipping contraband liquor, shouting over each other in their endless teasing and quips at each other's expense. A few others shared a meal at a nearby table. Two Delphians, bent over a computer screen, ignored everyone else. She approached the diners.

"At ease, soldiers," she joked. Although she outranked two of them, her lack of insignia was terribly inconvenient at this point.

They looked up when she spoke. "Where do you belong?" a young Centauri said when he did not recognize her. He smirked. "You can stay, though, if you're nice."

"The girl thinks she's a Caspian," a Human beside him said. "Where are your shoes?"

"Long story." Nova said. "And not very interesting. I'm looking for someone. Sethran Kada. Tall Centauri. Scar on his forehead. Longish hair."

"Oh, the *Dutchman*. Not seen him in a while. Was here earlier."

"Probably in the baths," another lieutenant said. "Those Centauri are part fish."

The Centauri corporal flapped her hands around his head. "Feel the slap of my fins, Human!"

Nova smiled and left them to go back out into the hall. She passed a few empty equipment rooms and the showers before turning around again. She was not eager to comb through the dorms for Seth and decided to wait by the *Dutchman* for his return.

"Hey!" she cried out when a strong hand clasped her arm and yanked her into one of the rooms lining the hallway. She found herself in a uniform locker, looking up at Seth.

"What are you doing down here?" He did not seem especially pleased to see her. He, like the others here, wore combat trousers, boots and a gray sleeveless shirt in spite of the cool air. And, unlike her, he seemed to fit well into this environment. Proving the pilot in the lounge correct, his hair was wet from a recent shower and a towel was slung around his neck. "Why did you leave the hospital?"

"They didn't want me there any more, believe me."

"You're shivering. That better just be because of the cold, not because you're sick." He motioned her to sit down to get her feet off the chilly floor. He straddled the bench beside her. "What did they find?"

"More than squid spit! There's a dead wanna-be nurse in my room who made it pretty clear that some folks want me gone."

"What happened!" he said, alarmed.

She told him in broad strokes about the diagnosis and the subsequent attack.

He listened with a furrowed brow. "Was the guy military?"

"Don't know. Had some physical training. Talked too much, though."

"Kada!" someone called from the hall.

Seth stood up when a pilot poked his head into the room. "There you are. Some to-do going on above," the sergeant said, regarding Nova curiously. "Some pilot's gone AWOL and they think she'll try to stow away and why am I not surprised to see you with someone that fits her description?"

Seth winked at Nova. "What else are they saying?"

"Not a thing, but Francis is monitoring. Sounds like they're awfully interested in finding her. They'll be all over us here before too long."

"I'm sure they're looking for someone else," Seth said. "This is my cousin."

Nova grimaced. "Funny guy." She stood up and followed Seth into the parking hall past the shuttles, cruisers and a few private planes to the *Dutchman*. He let her into the ship and locked the door behind her.

Not much later the sergeant arrived with two other pilots and a few boxes. One of them opened a portside access panel on the ship parked beside the *Dutchman* and quickly withdrew one of the outboard gun assemblies. He and one of the others began to tinker with it while the third pilot stood nearby with the type of sage advice usually offered by those not actually involved in the repair. Seth slouched on one of the boxes and sorted through some tools.

By the time the heavily-armed search detail appeared parts of the gun assembly lay scattered over a tarp at Seth's feet. The pilots maintained the arrogance usually displayed by airmen when in the company of ground crew and barely acknowledged the new arrivals.

"Evening," Seth said finally, busy with a caliper.

"Up a little late?" the guardsman asked.

"Is it?" one of Seth's companions asked. "I'm still on Feyd time. Could be next week for all I know."

"You flyboys haven't seen a female in hospital clothes hanging around, have you?" The group leader directed his inquiry at Seth. "For example, the one you brought onto the base yesterday?"

Seth shrugged. "Haven't seen her." He held a supply tube up for the guard's inspection. "What would you make of this, Sarge? Replace or repair?"

"You don't wonder why I'm looking for her?"

"If you need to find women in hospitals, then that's hardly my concern. I've had luck in the pilot ready room, personally." He smirked at the others. "Always someone ready in there."

The guard glowered and raised his voice over the rude laughter that followed Seth's remark. "So you don't mind if we had a look around your ship, then?"

"Yes, I mind, but I don't suppose I have a choice, do I?" Seth stood up and walked to the *Dutchman* where he placed his hand on its key plate. He returned to his seat without waiting for the gate to lower. "I'm so glad I tidied up in there," he said to the pilots. "Never know when company's coming."

The others laughed and returned to their tinkering.

* * *

Nova huddled in the airless plenum above the *Dutchman*'s cargo hold, wondering how much longer she'd be stuck in this dusty space, when she finally heard footsteps below. Then the thump and hiss of the ship's gate seal. After a moment a crack of light appeared on the floor as one of the tiles was lifted from below and pushed aside.

"Would you like to come down now?"

She slid to the opening and peered down at Seth. He held his arms up. She dangled her feet and let herself drop the short distance. He caught her, not without a smirk as she slid along his body before he lowered her to the floor.

"I think you still have some clothes here," he said when they went into the main cabin. "The stuff from Aikhor."

Nova went into the crew cabin to remove the stolen flight suit. He raised an eyebrow when she emerged, again wearing one of his shirts. She shivered and pulled the sleeves over her hands even though the temperature in the *Dutchman* was at a comfortable level.

"Are you all right?"

She dropped into one of the bucket chairs and drew her legs up onto it. "I'm not sure. Been one hell of a day."

"At the very least. Want some tea? Something a little stronger?"

"No, thanks. That was frightening up there." She pointed toward the ceiling. "Why didn't their scanners see me?"

"Dusted with an interesting mix of ordium and phenol. Confuses most measurements. Let me know if you get a rash."

"So you smuggle people, too?"

"Sometimes."

"Wonderful." She wrapped her arms around her knees. "I wish I knew what the hell is going on. Nothing is making any sense."

"Are you sure that nurse you killed was a rebel?"

She lifted her head. "He wasn't there to take my temperature! Said something about someone named Pe

Khoja sending him. From Magra. And a colonel."

He smiled grimly. "You're in terrible trouble."

"I kind of noticed that, Seth!" she exclaimed. "What's going on? What does that Pe Khoja want from me? And if you say 'classified' I'm going to kick you in the shin next time I have boots on!"

He hesitated a moment. "Pe Khoja hired us to take the box and get rid of your squad. He's obviously trying to finish the job. He is one of Tharron's people."

"I assumed Shri-Lan were involved in this. One of your friends?"

"I wouldn't say so. Although Pe Khoja leads the Arawaj faction. He's trying to organize a partnership with the Shri-Lan. That medic mentioned a colonel?"

"Didn't say which one. Just said that the colonel made sure that no one would help me here. Something like that."

He nodded. "I was wondering why Carras was so interested in you."

"What do you mean?" she said. "You're not suggesting that he was talking about Colonel Carras, are you?"

"I am. He's the only colonel stationed on Targon right now, mostly because of the Vanguard. The general runs the show here."

She jumped out of her chair. "That is absurd! Carras? That's just crazy. From what I've heard of him, he is a top-notch officer. Someone like that would rather chew glass than deal with rebels."

He grasped her arm before she had time to react. His fingers dug into her skin as he seemed to contemplate an urge to shake her. "Sometimes flyboys turn into rebels and colonels into traitors. Stop pretending that isn't so! Take your uniform off once in a while and see the real world, Nova! Those people tried to murder you today!"

She looked up into eyes that seemed to reflect every bit of light to burn into hers. There was none of his careless humor left in his expression. His patience had ended and there was no room for insolence and mockery. What she saw was a man who was desperately afraid for her life.

"I think I've been bruised up enough for one day," she said quietly.

He drew back and released her arms. "Sorry." He sighed. "Sorry. I just don't understand why you're so damn stubborn. You're acting like a first-year greenie. You know what goes on where people aren't looking. Why not here on Targon?"

"I'm AWOL, someone is trying to kill me and you just accused a high-ranking Union officer of treason. Probably the most important special ops officer in all of Trans-Targon. Can I please be upset about all that?"

"Think about it. Who knew you were coming here?"

Nova sank back into her chair, her eyes focused on nothing while she tried to make sense of his accusation. "I sent a message to my CO from Aikhor that I was going to try to get to Targon. She would have told them I was coming here. And probably what assignment I was on."

"And why would Carras care about a pilot that got stung by some xeno? That's what the doctors are for. And why would he be interested in some bit of piracy going on way past Zera? Happens every day out there. But alarm bells ring when the *Dyona* gets mentioned and he's practically sitting in your lap when you get here."

"But why?"

"That tank you were guarding seems to be worth an awful lot to someone. And now you are, too."

"And preferably dead."

"You have more to be upset about, while you're counting."

"Do tell."

"The nurse. You took his gun. And his key. And left him in your room. Dead."

"Wasn't going to ask him to dance."

"You're not just AWOL. You're a murderer. Whatever's floating around in your blood is important to them. To somebody. All of these are better reasons than desertion to launch a manhunt. Womanhunt."

"You're not funny. He was trying to kill me."

"Yes, but only you know that."

"Don't be absurd. Clearly..."

He waited.

"Well, they must know that... They'd know he doesn't belong there. Probably not even on the duty roster."

"It's a military hospital. Of course he would be."

"I'd have no reason to kill anyone in that place. I didn't even mean to kill him. He should have stayed down." She rubbed both of her hands over her face in a tired gesture. "I have to get to the general."

"And how would you to that? Knock on his bedroom door? You don't know who you can trust now. I think you should try to get a message to your father. Old Colonel Ironballs isn't going to let them play rough with his only begotten."

"No."

"What? Nova, there isn't anyone else you can turn to."

"This matter is classified," she said. "I am not prepared to accept that Carras is compromised. I know you think I'm naive, but it just doesn't sit right with me. There's obviously far more to this than he would tell some lieutenant he doesn't know. Who am I to question his orders?"

"You'd risk your life over that? You'd rather play soldier?"

"I *am* a soldier!" she snapped. After a moment she shifted her eyes away from his, feeling a little sheepish. "Well, and we had a fight."

"What about?"

"He said I had no regard for the chain of command." She slapped his arm when she saw the expression on his face. "Don't you laugh at me, Kada! I kinda went over someone's head on Bellac. It didn't go well. If I went to him now he would just order me to turn myself in to Carras. Desertion is not something he'd accept in the Whiteside clan."

He sighed and looked around the cabin as if to find

inspiration written on the bulkheads. "You have to leave this place, then. Get away until you can sort this out."

"How? I'll never get on a commuter now. Not with them looking for me. I don't know anybody here. There is no one I can trust." She suddenly felt tears burn in the back of her throat and bit them back, angry and unwilling to show how lost she felt. But the tension of this past hour had turned into fatigue and her mind felt as rubbery as her knees. "Except you."

"Yes, about as far as you can throw me, if I recall your current opinion of me." He ran his hands through his hair. "I need to know if *I* can trust *you*."

"Me?"

"Yes, *Lieutenant*," he said pointedly. "You know what I am. What I do. If I help you, can you leave the insignia behind?"

"I'm going AWOL. What does that tell you?"

"True. We'll leave in the morning."

"Let's go now!"

"That'll raise a flag. Technically, you're not AWOL for a few more hours." He took her hands to pull her to her feet and nudged her toward the lounger cubby tucked among the storage compartment and access panels in side of the cabin. "Come, lie down. You're exhausted."

She stiffened when he sat down on the daybed with her.

"You can trust me a little more," he said. "It's late. Just sleep a while. We're out of here in the morning."

Nova had to admit to herself, if not to him, that she so very much needed what he offered. Did he really know her so well? She put up only a token resistance when he pulled her down to lie beside him and wrapped her into a loose embrace. Basking in the warm comfort and sure safety of his presence, she sighed deeply. "Where are we going to go?"

"To see some rebels about a squid."

SIX

It wasn't until Nova switched the screens in the *Dutchman*'s cockpit to real-video that she realized they were approaching what she had always considered to be the wrong side of the planet.

"Magra Torley?" she said. "Not Magra Alaric?"

"What would I want on that continent?" Seth pretended to shudder. "Full of Union people and Union stuff and projectiles flying at me from Union pistols. Enough to make a person want to stay far far away."

She sighed. "All right, stop it. I should have realized you'd want Torley."

He began their descent over the continent that was less welcoming of Union members than other parts of the planet. While over the past three hundred years many of the habitable worlds in the Trans-Targon sector had come to at least tolerate an alliance with the Commonwealth, Magra had not. Perpetually at war with each other, three of the continents allowed access to Union members and took advantage of the benefits such alliance brought. The other two sided with the rebels and, in keeping Union presence from their shores, had become a haven for rebel activities.

"Try not to look like a lieutenant," Seth advised. "Don't you people know how to slouch?"

Nova sneered and went back into the cabin while he landed the *Dutchman* on a public airfield on the edge of Tanglan to change her clothes.

The past few days had been difficult for both of them. The *Dutchman* had not been searched again before given clearance to leave Targon and they had set course for the jumpsite back toward Magra without incident. But some awkwardness seemed to have settled between them, perhaps because of the hours they had spent asleep together on his bed. Too many memories had crept in there with them and both of them now took painstaking care to avoid speaking of those, avoid touching, avoid even looking at the other for too long.

Nova put it aside as an aberrant moment of weakness and set her sights on solving the mystery that had come into her life along with the poison delivered to her hospital room. If Seth's contacts could offer no clues about what had happened to her on the *Dyona* and why the pirates were sent to retrieve the tank, she would present herself to the base on Magra Alaric. She would face the consequences of whatever had happened on Targon and let her commanders deal with assassins and rebel infiltrations. This whole situation was intolerable. Her defiance went against everything she had been taught, that she believed in, and that she had trained for.

She waited until the *Dutchman* had settled to the ground before reaching for her medication. Between the long periods she spent asleep, conserving energy, and the drugs given to her by Doctor Darshan she felt almost perfectly healthy.

"Must you do this where I have to watch?" Seth had come into the cabin.

She injected one of the ampoules into her arm. "Did you ever think you might be in the wrong line of work, seeing how squeamish you get about things?" She counted the remaining vials in her package of medicine. "I'm a bit worried about running out of this stuff."

"Take some with you. Maybe we can find it here."

She tucked one of the vials into a pocket of the leather vest she had filched from him and reached up to loosen the tight chignon at her nape to let her hair fall freely over her shoulders. Her snug breeches were tucked into solid boots and the rail gun lashed to her thigh added what she hoped was an aura of menace to her appearance. "So do I look like a rebel?"

"I don't think it should be anyone's goal to look like a rebel. In fact, most rebels try very hard not to look like rebels."

"Don't spoil my fun."

"Well, just don't start shooting people," he said. "This is a neutral planet and you have no authority here. We're not here to hunt rebels. You can do that on Union time, not while you're AWOL."

Nova followed him out of the *Dutchman* and onto the airfield which was little more than a paved surface among rolling expanses farmland. She was curiously disoriented by the vast tracts of vegetation reaching to the horizon. The skyranches she had seen were orderly rings of multi-level hydroponic production units and she had only a vague concept of how animals might be used for food. Seth had to grin when she stopped to stare at a four-legged creature behind a low fence. The massive, horned animal would surely not be stopped by such a flimsy barrier should it be moved to charge at them. Yet it seemed content to return her gaze, chewing on whatever there was to be found on the ground. "Leave your gun where it is, Nova," Seth said. "That's not a rebel."

She let him pull her along. "It's so huge! What is it?"

"Dinner, hopefully," he said. "I could really use some real food for a change. With luck we'll get fed when we get to the lab."

"People eat that? Look at those eyes!"

He had to laugh. "You can tell an M-track from a trap rail at fifty paces but you've never seen a live daram? They're great with mushrooms. That's fungus."

"I know what mushrooms are, wise guy."

They walked onward, toward a scatter of houses along the country road, each surrounded by gardens and orchards. A cool breeze blew from nearby hills but the sun shone warmly and Nova enjoyed the stroll. "Actually prettier here than over on Alaric," she said. "So where is this lab?"

"Right there." He pointed to one of the cottages along the tree-lined road. Modern additions had been added to the original stone building over time and as the need arose, turning it into a sprawling compound. Behind it stood several greenhouses.

The door to the main house opened before they had even reached it. "Sethran, you shiftless vagrant! About time you visited again!" An elder Terran came outside, his arms raised in greeting. He clapped Seth's back in a loose embrace. "I told Acie that she was dreaming when she told me you sent a message!"

"Good to see you, Vincent. This is Nova Whiteside that I mentioned in my packet."

The old man studied her for an uncomfortably long interval. "So you think it's wise to bring one of them here?"

"No choice, I'm afraid. She's our specimen."

"Well, I trust your judgment. Come inside." He waved them into the house. "Have you eaten? Acie! They're here! Now where did that girl get to? Come, let's have tea. Or would you prefer something else, Miss Whiteside? I have some wine. Very good, too. Perhaps you'll join me in a glass. Too bad that Sethran doesn't indulge."

Nova had been looking around the entrance of the cottage, charmed by its blend of rustic materials and modern conveniences. "He doesn't?"

"Tea's fine," Seth said as they walked into the kitchen. "Hello, Acie."

Nova turned to see a small woman enter through the rear

door of the house. Unmistakably Bellac, her skin was of a deep red contrasting with the long braids of startling white hair gathered into a thick ponytail. She wore a loose shift and carried a basket of produce. "Seth! You made it. I heard you had some trouble back there."

"A little."

Nova scrutinized the woman more closely. "Don't I know you?"

Acie smiled broadly and put the basket onto the thick slab of wood that served as a table in the middle of the room. "We all look the same to you, don't we?"

"Not to me. I lived on Bellac for months. You're the... woman we saw on Aikhor!"

Seth nodded. "Meet Acie Daruen, an expert chemist and squash grower. The tail was just decorative." He grinned at Vincent. "Perhaps Nova will have the wine."

"Yes, and then I'll make dinner. I have a very nice bird all ready to go."

"We probably shouldn't stay long," Seth said. "Why don't you go bleed for Acie, Nova, so she can start whatever tests need to get done?"

Acie waved Nova along, out of the kitchen. Nova followed, a little baffled by all that was going on. They walked through a cozy commons room filled with overstuffed furniture and piles of books, 3D's and reader tablets everywhere. Among them lolled several small animals that she might have seen in illustrations somewhere. The Bellac opened a door and walked ahead of Nova into a basement level instantly illuminated when they stepped into the stairwell.

A small but gleaming and modern laboratory awaited them at the bottom of the stairs. Nova turned in the small space, seeing spotless counters and equipment, coolers, heaters, things that spun and things that contained tiny rodents.

"Nice," she commented.

"Well, it's home. I've got a few experiments already

started. Come, have a seat here and roll up a sleeve. And fill me in."

Nova complied and bared her arm for Acie's needle. "We were transporting a cephalopod of some sort in a water ash matrix. It stung me before it died. The doctors on Targon suspect it was carrying some sort of organism but they don't know why. It's not native to the species."

The Bellac removed a vial of blood and attached another. "I know all that. Fill me in on you and Seth!"

Nova coughed. "Seth?"

"Yah."

Nova frowned. "We used to be friends. Long ago. How about you fill me in about *you* and Seth. What was that back there on Aikhor?"

Acie shrugged. "We were meeting there to take the lab out. Been planned for months although he was a few days late because of some other job. I was there to see if there was anything useful we needed to remove or that shouldn't be just blown into the sky. We found a few things and put those on his ship. Unfortunately, there was someone working late at the lab and then a bottle of something that Centauri don't tolerate so well got broken. Well, sort of thrown at him. We got the job done but Seth was just ill the whole time. So I took him back to the inn. Poor guy had trouble seeing straight!" She laughed at the memory. "Here, exhale into this as hard as you can."

"He let me believe he was drunk!"

"Oh," she said. "Oops. I talk too much."

"I'm getting used to being left in the dark," Nova grumbled. She blew into a tube as instructed. "That was quite the outfit you were almost wearing."

"Well, we all use what we've got, honey," Acie said with the same breathy warble she had used on Aikhor. Nova could not help but join her laughter.

"Okay, got enough," Acie announced. She opened a metal cabinet and crouched low to search through some containers. "I'm going to start playing with water ash, so you better go in case those doctors are wrong about you being immune. Close the door at the top of the stairs. It'll seal. Let me know when dinner is ready."

Nova left the diminutive Bellac in her lab and made her way back upstairs. She heard gentle laughter from the direction of the kitchen.

"I thought she was going to shoot the poor daram," Seth was saying. Nova smiled when Vincent replied with more laughter.

"So does she know who you are?" he said, suddenly sounding very sober. Nova stopped in mid-stride. "Who we are? This could be dangerous to us all."

"I trust her. You want to relocate the lab soon, anyway. I'll cover our tracks once she's back where she belongs."

"She could be useful to us. Especially now, with you so close."

"She is Air Command and always will be. I won't risk her getting mixed up in this any more than necessary." He was silent for a moment. "I just can't."

"If she's not one of us she's as dangerous to you as you are to her. Don't get caught up with her, son."

"Well, I had my chance and I blew it a long time ago. Don't worry about that."

Nova bent to pet one of the animals that roamed the cottage, cooing loudly enough for the two men in the kitchen to hear. She entered the room. "That little black thing is so sweet. Please tell me that isn't breakfast."

"Oh, no, Acie would carve me up into thin slices if anything happened to little Maru. Will you taste some of these roasted pepper pods, Miss Whiteside?"

"Nova," she said. "I don't think anyone has ever called me 'Miss' before." She took a seat at the high table. Something simmering in a nearby pot was filling the kitchen with mouth-watering aroma and she inhaled deeply. "I'd love a taste, sir."

"Only if you call me Vincent. I take it that Acie has settled into her beakers and gadgets by now?"

Nova nodded. "That is a very nice lab down there. For such a remote location." She smiled at the Human. "I won't pry, don't worry. I'm grateful that you are willing to help me with my problem. Forget who I am." She glanced at Seth. "And I won't ask who you are."

"Well, that's probably for the best, then," Vincent said brightly. "Now, until our dinner is ready, how about a tour of our lovely garden?"

"Seen it," Seth said. "What I'd really like is to stand in a hot shower for a while."

"Me, too!" Nova said at once. "Um, after you, I mean. Your *Dutchman*'s system is adequate, but nothing beats buckets and buckets of water."

"Please, make yourself at home," Vincent said. "There is no shortage of sunshine on Magra. The cells are fully charged and the tanks are right up with lovely hot water."

A few enjoyable hours followed. Acie joined them for dinner but even while the others ate and talked she was busy with her little screens and notes and didn't seem to notice that there were two pencils tucked behind her ears. She disappeared back into the basement before the others had even finished their meal. Nova listened to the stories and chatter around the table, feeling wholly at ease in the overheated kitchen with its clutter of dishes, glasses and bottles strewn over the table among a growing pile of books and tablets. The conversation rambled through distant places and foreign worlds that interested Vincent as much as they did Seth. He clearly deferred to the older man and she noticed none of the irreverence that colored his speech at other times. It had been a long while since Nova had felt as comfortable and untroubled as she did in this company.

It was well past midnight before they heard the seal to the basement door hiss gently in preparation of opening.

"Ah, here is our mad scientist," Vincent declared. "While I won't pretend that we are better equipped than those vast facilities on Targon, Acie does have a way of ferreting things out."

"For sure she does." All of them turned when the Bellac stepped into the kitchen. She lifted a hand and drizzled a handful of amber dust onto the surface of the wooden table.

"What's this?" Vincent said.

"That, my friends, is water ash."

They sat in stunned silence, looking at the scatter of dust like it might leap up and turn into some monster of profound proportions.

Acie laughed. "Or what's left of it. Totally inert. Useless. Non-poisonous. Might as well be wood ash."

Seth poked a finger at the dust. "How did you figure this out?"

"Took nothing more than to mix a little of Nova's blood with the ash in the absence of air. I still don't know what exactly is in the blood to make this happen, but that isn't the question here, is it?"

"The question is why," Nova said.

"Precisely. And you can bet it didn't take your Union doctors any longer than me to figure this out." She turned Nova's wrist and pointed to the blue lines under her skin. "It's a catalyst. What I don't know is why anyone would want to create something to counter water ash properties. Ash is rare, it's expensive, and it's very useful for all sorts of things from drugs to weapons."

"This catalyst could be useful in an emergency," Vincent suggested. "You can neutralize the poisonous effects of a water ash containment failure, maybe."

"No. As soon as you expose Nova's blood to air, the agent loses its cohesion with the hijacked hemoglobin and also becomes inert. I suspect it was made with some sort of plant matter. In any case, the catalyst won't work in an oxygen-rich environment. Which is precisely what most of us like to live in. I can't imagine this stuff is easy to create and we all know it's not easy to transport."

"Sabotage," Nova said. "You can use this to destroy someone's stockpile of water ash. Or even a source of it." She looked around the table. "The Commonwealth holds most of the accessible water ash resources. It's what makes us powerful. A catalyst like this would cause far more damage to the money supply than blowing up a base or an arsenal."

"Rebels, you mean," Seth said.

"Didn't you say that Tharron has labs everywhere? They could be whipping this up."

"I don't think this is the work of any of the rebel factions," Vincent said. "My theory is that a competitor is scheming to harm the Union's supply of water ash. The Commonwealth is a big player, but there are others like the Callas conglomerate or even Sadon Corp who compete with the Commonwealth. Some of their dealings with the Union have been bitter."

"Makes sense," Seth said. He turned to Nova. "Don't forget that Pe Khoja ordered the hit on the *Dyona*. And the hit on you, on Targon. He's working with Tharron. So he's trying to get his hands on the box because it's valuable, or he's trying to stop the catalyst from getting to where it's going."

"You're forgetting something," Acie said. "Didn't you say earlier that the catalyst was sent by Delphians? I can't imagine any Delphian with a reason to want to work with Sadon Corp. Or the Commonwealth on a commercial project. Or rebels, especially. You need to find those Delphians if we're ever going to know why this was created and where it was going."

"Delphians who are *not* likely to be rebels," Seth said with a meaningful glance at Nova. "No such thing as a Delphian rebel."

"None you know of," she said, unwilling to concede the point. But he was right. Isolated on their comfortable planet, Delphians had little need for anything the Commonwealth so tantalizingly held out to less wealthy worlds. They were simply not for sale, although they applied their superior brains to what causes they found interesting or deserving.

Vincent placed his hand over Nova's to give it a gentle

squeeze. "One doesn't have to be a rebel to oppose the dealings of your mighty Commonwealth of United Planets, Lieutenant. Let's dispense with labels. Tharron's dreadful followers are truly rebels of the worst sort. But perhaps others just don't want to be part of your Union." He put his other hand on Acie's. "Acie lost her home during the invasion of Bellac. Sethran tells me you were there. Just because you liberated them does not make them your subjects. Or even Union loyalists."

Nova nodded. "I have to admit things seem a lot simpler if you're just told where to point your gun. Or so Seth keeps telling me." She reached into her pocket and withdrew one of her medicine capsules. "I am going to run out of this soon." She handed it to Acie. "And when I do I will have to go back, whether I want to or not."

Acie peered at the information shown in minute script on the ampoule. "They'll have to hold the court martial a while longer. I think I can get this batched up for you. Not here in Tanglan but up the coast a bit. There's a dispensary in Naos." She looked up at Seth. "Past the temple road by Joel's place. Might take a few days, though."

"I don't want to be on Magra that long," Seth said. "We'll trip over to Pelion to see what we can find and then come back here."

"We should all be that wealthy," Vincent said. "You must be using up coolant like water."

"I am. Meanwhile, I need you to do something." Seth pointed a thumb at Nova. "My co-pilot pretty much shredded her career when she stepped off Targon. Can you get on the grapevine and spread a few rumors? Let it be known that she was taken by rebels. Maybe held for ransom or prisoner exchange or something." He grinned. "Nothing too dramatic. I'm starting to feel sorry for her old man and I don't even like the guy."

SEVEN

Few could argue that Feyd, a planet tucked safely among easily-accessible, well-charted and well-guarded jumpsites, offered a veritable paradise to most species that valued veritable paradises.

Colonel Drackon gazed through the transparent dome of the skimmer to see rolling hills of vegetation and open, untouched meadows as they sped smoothly over little-used traffic lanes into open country. Only the barely tolerable temperatures and airborne allergens kept outsiders from overrunning this planet, something for which, Drackon suspected, the native Feydans were grateful.

He turned to glance at the driver of the air car.

"Factor," he said, as always uncomfortable in the presence of any of the Elected Ten and especially this one. "As much as I like a drive in the countryside..."

"Just enjoy the view, Colonel. Look at those vineyards. The genes in those grapes come all the way from your home world and here they are, growing past all expectation in this climate. Best wine anywhere."

Drackon sighed, resigned to the Factor's penchant for keeping him tethered on some imaginary leash for as long as possible before getting to the point. Obedient to his master's wishes, he admired the rows of vines stretching across the hills. His eyes also took in the air car in front of him and the two sleds just behind and to the side. While Rellius had chosen to drive alone with Drackon, his bodyguards were never completely out of sight.

He wondered if any of the other Ten were aware of Rellius' current projects. One did not create a Commonwealth of this magnitude without making compromises, but would anyone sanction the sort of compromises they were now making? And did one rise into the ranks of the Elected Ten without sacrificing principle for the sake of expedience?

"I do so love the country," Rellius breathed deeply of the filtered and cooled air inside the dome. As usual, Drackon was unsure of the Centauri's sarcasm; his dislike for Feyd as the Commonwealth's seat of commercial ventures was no secret. Other Factors oversaw Union military, cultural, scientific and civil matters from residences scattered over several planets here in Trans-Targon as well as in the distant Centauri sector. Feyd's location within the jumpgate web was the obvious choice for this Factor's base. Rellius thumbed a control on the car's dashboard to drop the temperature further.

"Now, about Tharron," he said. "Report?"

Drackon blinked, startled out of his thoughts. "Yes, sir. The Shri-Lan are still holding the sub-sector that houses the breach to Naiya. In overall charge of that is Tharron's newest henchman, a Caspian named Pe Khoja on Magra. Their demands are growing."

Rellius nodded. "Both a blessing and a curse, those pesky rebels, aren't they?" He followed the lead car and turned into a forested area. Dappled shade from above turned the interior of the air car into a flickering confusion of light and shadow. "Too bad they found out about the breach, but their blockade is more effective than anything we can explain without drawing attention to that piece of nothing out there.

What do they want now?"

"I received a message from Pe Khoja just yesterday. They want ten thousand flash modules or they'll hand the coordinates over to Sadon Corp."

At another time Drackon might have found it amusing to listen to the invective now spewing across the Factor's lips upon hearing about this development. Losing Naiya and its wealth of water ash to their main competitor would deal a serious blow to Union interests. As a career soldier, the logistics of trade bedeviling the Commonwealth interested him not the least. This time, however, there was as much at stake for him as there was for Rellius.

"Are we nowhere close to finishing the job out at Naiya?" Rellius said once he had muttered the last of his expletives. "I am getting tired of pandering to Tharron, no matter how convenient he might be right now."

"I have some very good people on that, sir, but we don't have a Level Three spanner out there. Those tend to be Delphian and we aren't likely to get one of them working with us on this project. Without someone with that skill, every charting trip through the breach is costing a fortune and exhausts one of our spanners for a day, at least. It will still be a few more weeks before we have completed the calculations and the site is stable."

"Expedite it! Get a better spanner somewhere! There has to be a hungry one out there looking for a job. If not, persuade one of them in whatever way you see fit. They're abnormally fond of their families. Use that. Just find one stat!"

"Yes, Factor," Drackon said.

"Send the damn modules. Whatever. I'll have them released to you for your campaign in the Mrak sector. Reroute them to Pe Khoja. But this has got to end. Soon. I'll not have Tharron hold the entire project hostage."

"Yes, Factor."

"I want you out there, too."

"Me, sir?"

"Show a little muscle. They are getting far too belligerent. We are in charge of that platform, not Tharron and his lackeys. And most of all, light a fire under your damn spanners to finish those charts. I want the first ships going into Naiya by the next assembly of Factors. I need something to place before my esteemed colleagues. What's better than the financial security of this entire sector?"

"Yes, sir," the colonel said, mentally rearranging his schedule to make a trip into the Badlands plausible. He'd have to take a cruiser and go little-armed into what was now essentially rebel-held territory near the breach to Naiya. Why had he even gotten out of bed this morning?

"If you can accomplish this, Sam, I will be that much more inclined to get you off this planet and onto Targon where you belong. My recommendation will go a long way to seeing you replace Tal Carras there. You're as close to making general as he is. I think having you there will serve both of us much better in the future, don't you?"

"Most certainly, sir," the colonel replied, inwardly ecstatic. It had been a while since the Factor had so directly addressed Drackon's ultimate ambition. Once based on Targon, few things stood in his way to direct Air Command's efforts to his liking. Carras not only led the Vanguard squadron but also most major tactical operations originating there. It represented power that was surpassed only by a tedious collection of generals and the Factors themselves. But it would take the support of a Factor to unseat Carras and take that commission for himself.

"Now fill me in on our other problem," Rellius said. "That little girl with the nasty case of hypoxia."

Drackon ground his teeth, uneager to share more bad news with the Factor, especially now. "She... has disappeared, sir."

Rellius slowed the skimmer and allowed it to settle gently to the ground. The escort vehicles around them did the same. He took his time in powering down before half-turning in his seat to look at his subordinate. Drackon realized that he was sitting far too close to the Centauri, a design flaw of the skimmer that until today had not bothered him.

"Report," Rellius said, barely controlling his voice.

"As you know, she was hospitalized on Targon for testing. They discovered the properties of the catalyst but had not taken steps to remove it, according to my sources. The implications of this substance are of course far-reaching and Carras knows it. He plans to defer the matter to the Factors once more is known about it. We tried to eliminate the woman but she eluded your agent. Killed him, in fact. She is currently listed as AWOL."

"AWOL on Targon?"

"We don't know. Targon is riddled with cave systems. There are entire communities living underground, including rebels. She could also have left the planet on an outbound ship that day."

Rellius tipped his head against the backrest of his seat and closed his eyes. A long wave of his black hair hung over his eyes and he blew it forcefully back over his forehead.

An uncomfortable silence followed while Drackon stared out of the window at the Factor's guards. They balanced casually on their sleds, apparently not interested in why their employer had stopped in this remote patch of forest. Drackon had sometimes fancied that these expressionless, silent men and women were perhaps cleverly-designed mechanical beings – those here today did not even seem affected by Feyd's oppressive heat.

"Sir," he said cautiously. "As long as she's invisible, no one can get at the catalyst. Any blood sample they still have from her would be useless by now."

Rellius waved his assurances aside with a weak gesture. "I am surrounding myself with people who can't rob a cargo freighter without losing the objective, can't control a handful of rebels in the middle of nowhere and who can't manage to capture an unarmed woman in a hospital bed. How am I *not* supposed to despair at this moment, Colonel?"

"We may have underestimated her."

The Factor leaned forward to start the skimmer again. "She'll try to contact her father, Colonel Whiteside. Make sure you stay on top of that. Then find her. Eliminate her. Don't fail me again. Am I clear?"

"Yes, sir," Drackon said without letting his resentment show. The agent sent to take care of the woman had been one of Rellius' own Prime Staff. Untraceable, unknown, surely a puzzle at Carras' hands right now. Why was the blame now his?

Rellius turned the skimmer back toward Talan An. "What about the Delphian lab?"

"We believe it to be on one of the Pelion moons. It will be eliminated within days."

"Why am I less confident of that than you seem to be?"

EIGHT

"You sure this is it?" Seth peered up at the metal building over the top of his respirator. They were faced by an endless expanse of wall leading to an airfield in the distance. Shuttles and small cargo frigates appeared and disappeared behind the building, indicating a busy shipping concern. There were no windows on the massive warehouse but a jumble of signs in many languages promised a plethora of goods for sale and trade.

"Yeah, only Humans can build something this ugly," Nova said and shifted the oxygen tank slung over her back. "I miss Magra," she added with a smile. A cold and abrasive wind riffled through their clothing and she wished she had worn a few more layers.

He scanned the wide traffic lane beside the building. It was a dusty scrape of bare rock dividing rows of similar warehouses and manufactories. Skimmers and sleds hovered noiselessly along this highway but there were few people on foot. Pelion offered lovely and livable areas to those who could breathe the air; this was not one of them. The constant air traffic here made the assembly of a dome to accommodate other species impractical.

Seth pulled on a small door next to a sign promising safe and prompt shipping to many destinations. They entered a metal-walled and dust-covered service area. It displayed little more than a weighing platform and a conveyor leading into the rear of the building. The sound of voices and of shipping containers being handled by rails and wheeled trolleys echoed somewhere in the rear halls of the building. Here, too, the walls were covered in signs as well as price lists and insurance notices.

Nova leaned over the conveyor. "Waiter!"

It took several minutes before a Human in coveralls ambled from the back to greet his newest customers. "Help you?" he said, most of his attention on Nova's legs. Instead of a full respirator, the additional oxygen he needed was fed to him by two slim tubes inserted into his nose. Probably more comfortable in the long run, thought Nova.

"Looking for a shipper," Seth said. "A Delphian. You get many Delphians around here?"

"Not often," the man said. "Got a name?"

"No. You took a shipment a couple of days ago, bound for Magra on the *Dyona*."

The clerk raised his hands to ward off this inquiry. "Not my problem. Ship got robbed. They had their own insurance."

"I'm not interested in insurance. I need to speak to the Delphian."

Nova hopped up onto the conveyor and idly picked up a wad of wrap used to secure containers onto their pallets. "Brought in a box about this big. Tempered glass. Yellow stuff in it." She held out her hands to describe the tank in the air.

"You can't sit on that. We don't give out information about our customers."

"Except to rebel agents?"

The Human squinted at them suspiciously. "Who's asking?"

Seth glanced at Nova as if surprised by the question. "We

are. Do you see anyone else here?"

"Look, Centauri. You two be on your way. I've got nothing for you."

Seth's hand shot out to grasp the man's ear and pull his head down onto the conveyor before he had time to react. Nova placed her boot heel onto his neck. Seth took her wad of wrapping and stuffed it into the man's mouth.

The clerk shouted into his gag, eyes wide. Seth placed his gun to the Human's nape when Nova removed her foot and slid off the conveyor to peer through the door leading into the back halls.

"I think maybe if I removed that stuff you're choking on you might be able to give us a name and address?" Seth asked politely.

The man screamed again.

Seth looked over to Nova. "Red, since he's one of your people, would you mind terribly if I broke his arm?"

"Can I watch?"

He grinned and tipped his head toward a computer screen mounted on the wall. Nova activated it.

"Batch number," Seth said to the clerk. "Or your arm. Choose."

The clerk nodded fervently, no longer interested in protecting his clientele. Seth pulled out the gag and the man rattled off a series of numbers that Nova entered into the computer. Seth replaced the gag and leaned on the man's back while he watched Nova.

She tapped her way through recent records until she found the date she looked for. Among the entries to be found there was the one for the *Dyona*. The payload listed a box destined for Magra and the name beside it sounded Delphian. "This must be it. HazMat shipment, armed escort. Sent by someone Celessa. No other name. On Tyra. Got the coordinates."

Seth turned his attention back to the clerk. "You know, there is something that interests us. When you were asked to arrange for a Union escort, who did you contact other than the base on Zera?"

The man shook his head, looking even more panicked.

"Come on, you can tell us. We haven't even broken your arm yet."

The clerk closed his eyes in resignation and went limp. Seth removed the gag again. "I was told to send a message to Magra. Some guy named Zizzy."

Seth looked up at Nova. "Pe Khoja's flunky." He gently squeezed the trigger of his gun. The man's body jerked briefly and then collapsed. "He'll be out for a while but we don't have much time."

Nova helped him shift the clerk to the floor and push him under the weigh scale, out of sight of the casual observer. "We need to find some weather gear for you," Seth said. "I don't think I have anything that'll fit you. Let's try one of the trading places elsewhere in case someone here gets nosy."

* * *

It was not long until Seth brought the *Dutchman* down onto Tyra, one of Pelion's moons. Its orange surface boasted little more than a scattering of mining facilities, some dilapidated to the point of safety hazard, and a convenient dump for Pelion's more dangerous waste products. Seth and Nova climbed into pressure suits for the walk to the buildings listed on the shipper's waybill.

"Have you had much to do with Delphians?" Seth asked as they were preparing to leave the ship. He placed her helmet onto her neck plate and waited for the sensors to confirm a seal before bending to let her help him with his own gear.

"Not a lot." She watched him lift a gloved hand to signal that he heard her over their com system. "Snooty bunch. I don't think they like Humans very much."

"Well, they don't really like anybody who isn't from Delphi. Isolationists, the lot of them. But their huge brains just won't let them stay put. Ever since the Union got to this part of the galaxy, they've been crazy about exploration."

"Seems like a bit of a contradiction."

"It makes sense to them. We need them more than they need us. So they get to play with our toys while pretending to be above such trifles. No wonder people think they're, um, snooty."

"But you don't?" Nova activated the controls to depressurize the cargo bay after checking to make sure that everything in the small chamber was securely fastened.

"They're not so bad once you get to know them. Be sure to treat them politely. They like that."

"I'm always polite."

He snorted in derision and nudged her onto the ramp. They walked slowly toward a single-storied metal box seemingly dropped at random into the moistureless landscape. Other buildings, mostly domed, appeared to belong to the miners. A few transporters parked nearby but no one was about. A camera above the hatch of what they assumed to be the Delphian lab followed them as they approached. Seth waved at it.

"So how do you know they'll even want to talk to us?" Nova said, awkwardly twisting in her suit to look around the barren moon.

"Yes," a cool voice issued from the speakers in their helmets. "How do you?"

Seth hummed thoughtfully. "How about: we have your catalyst? Courtesy of one Myrid passenger aboard the *Dyona*."

Nova snickered when she heard the connection pop in her ear as someone in the building cut their com link. Just a few moments later the light above the door blinked to indicate depressurization. They were inside a few minutes later and peeling out of their suits when the interior door opened to admit a tall, blue-haired woman wearing coveralls.

"Welcome to our castle," she said, but there was neither welcome nor humor in her expression. "You can imagine that we are intrigued by your news about the catalyst." She stood aside to let them enter the building. Nova looked up at the woman as they passed and was met by sapphire eyes a few shades darker than the startling silvery-blue hair hanging board-straight to her shoulders. More closely related to the Centauri than Humans, these people looked much like their black-haired cousins, but bore none of their charm. Nova wondered if the Delphian felt as cold as she looked.

They found themselves in a bare-bones laboratory peopled by three more Delphians hunched over their benches. Like all Delphian males, the men wore their hair much longer than the females, gathered in a tidy braid. They looked up from their work but seemed content to let the woman deal with the visitors.

"You are Celessa?" Nova asked. "My name is Nova Whiteside and that is Sethran Kada. Your catalyst has been a little problematic for us."

The Delphian motioned them into an alcove away from the work benches where they sat on inflatable loungers covered by thin blankets. There were few pieces of furniture here; mostly lightweight folding equipment used on remote outposts where shipping any piece of luxury was an expensive venture. Despite the frugal accommodations, everything here was spotless and tidy.

"We assumed it lost," Celessa said. "They told us the ship was destroyed. How did you come into possession of the catalyst?"

"I was aboard the *Dyona*," Nova explained. "As part of the escort. I'm sorry that I was unable to protect the tank. It was broken during the attack."

"So where is the catalyst, then?"

"In there," Seth jerked his chin into Nova's direction. "Your Myrid stung her and transferred the agent."

The Delphian's pale lips actually shifted into a smile as she considered the possibility. She raised her hands toward Nova and then dropped them again. "But that's... that's just wonderful news! Please, may I check for the presence of the agent?"

"We've already tested it. It turns water ash into so much junk."

"Please, indulge me. This is very exciting for us."

Nova sighed and pushed her sleeve up. "Kind of tired of being poked with sharp things, but go ahead," she said.

The Delphian rushed back into the main lab to confer with her colleagues.

"I've never seen a Delphian quite so animated," Seth said. "Let's hope they have a way of getting rid of this thing for you."

Celessa returned a few moments later. "Please, Elder Sister, this way."

Nova turned back to Seth as they followed the Delphian into a narrow hallway. "Elder sister?" she hissed.

"You should be pleased. They don't often call outsiders that."

Celessa led them into a separate lab which contained a transparent tank connected to a tangle of hoses. The door sealed behind them. Another Delphian was busy with the box into which he now carefully placed a small, covered bowl.

"All right," Seth said. "Why does *he* get to wear a respirator?"

The Delphian smiled, for the second time. "Just a precaution. His name is Kiely. If you don't mind, Shan Whiteside, I need you to bleed into that bowl after we seal the container. It's the closest we can get to simulating an *in situ* experiment."

Nova followed her direction to insert her arm into a tight valve on the side of the box and hold her hand just above the bowl. Celessa did the same from the other side and picked up a scalpel that her colleague had placed in the box. A fan whirred alive somewhere nearby to draw the air out of the container. "Not to worry, we're just replacing oxygen with a neutral gas similar to what is found on Naiya."

"What's Naiya?"

"A planet in the Outlands. Where we had intended the

box to go. Ready?" Celessa removed the lid from the bowl of water ash in the tank.

"I guess," Nova grumbled, her eyes on the scalpel.

"Want me to hold your hand?" Seth whispered.

She playfully kicked his leg just as Celessa sliced her blade across the pad of one of Nova's fingers. "Put that finger right into the water ash."

"What?"

Celessa took Nova's hand and pushed it into the bowl. They all leaned forward to watch as the amber powder absorbed the liquid from Nova's hand and a discoloration expanded from the insignificant wound. They heard a hissing, crackling sound lasting just a few seconds.

"Now what?"

Celessa nodded to the other Delphian. "Now we think it's inert. If the catalyst you carry is actually viable."

Kiely crouched beside the box to reach into the cabinet below the tank. The floor of the box opened and the bowl dropped out of sight. Celessa picked up a bottle and rinsed the powder and blood from Nova's fingers. They heard another hiss when Kiely replaced the gas inside the chamber with air. "No ash remains in the container," he said after checking his data display. He spoke Delphian, a language both Seth and Nova understood. "I require some moments to analyze the sample."

Celessa released the tight valves around her own and Nova's arms.

"You can imagine that we're curious about why you want to neutralize water ash," Nova said. "Especially since it's such a convoluted process."

Celessa nodded and beckoned them to leave the lab with her. "You ought to know. Let me introduce you to the Naiyad."

They returned to the hall and entered another room, this one so dimly lit that they had to take a moment to accustom themselves after the bright light outside. The most prominent object in the room was a large tank filled with the amber fluid that was not quite water and not quite powder. Even as they approached it they could see movements inside.

"This looks familiar," Nova said.

"This is a Naiyad. As was the being in the tank we sent. They are closely related to Myrids and so that is what we declared when we asked for an escort. This is the last Naiyad we have here."

Nova and Seth approached the tank for a closer look at the creature. It hovered near the glass and they saw two large, lidless eyes stare back at them. The Naiyad's skin was a pebbled tan but the underside of the boneless limbs shifted from shades of pink and purple to blue as it moved. This tank allowed for more movement than the small shipping container had and they noticed that some of the limbs ended in three finger-like appendages. It tapped those against the inside of the box in a rhythmic pattern.

"She's acknowledging your presence," Celessa said. "They use touch to communicate even very complex messages. We have not been able to decipher much of it."

"Clever of you to ask for help from Air Command to get these shipped around," Nova said, resisting an urge to tap the glass in return.

The Delphian frowned. "We should have tried to find the funds for a direct flight. Something less attractive to pirates. But the best we could afford was a captain of a private ship on Magra. He would not come into Pelion space. So that's when we decided to just hire a shipping company. But their transport was substandard, as was the guard they hired for the job."

Nova started to object but Seth had placed a hand on her arm. "It appears the shipper contacted some... rebels who had probably been waiting for just such a shipment to leave this area."

Celessa's delicate brow furrowed and she observed Seth like a particularly simple-minded lab creature. "Don't be absurd, Centauri. We may be naive when it comes to knowing how to ship a Naiyad across Trans-Targon, but we know very well what is at stake. They were waiting for exactly *this* shipment to be sent out. Your Colonel Drackon has done everything short of searching every moon over Pelion to try to shut us down. Call him a rebel if you wish; he's far worse than that."

"Colonel Drackon!" Nova exclaimed. "That's the commander of the Union base on Feyd. How would he be involved in all... this?" Her gesture included not only the tank here in the room but the laboratory as well. "And why?"

"Son of a Rhuwac." Seth smiled grimly.

She squinted up at him. "What do you know about this?"

"About this? Nothing. About Drackon? Plenty. Pe Khoja has been working with him. At least that's what we... I've been suspecting."

"What? You're saying that Colonel Drackon is a rebel?"

"I am. Or at least in bed with them."

"How can you be sure of that? What does he want?" Nova's question was for Celessa. "Why does he care about these... these Naiyads?"

"At this point I imagine he wants you. He is looking to destroy the catalyst. I'll tell you what we know." Celessa raised her hands to place them onto a metal plate on the side of the tank. The creature drifted toward her and brushed its undulating limbs against the inside. The Delphian closed her eyes. A few minutes passed in silence.

"The Naiyad is asking who you are," she said finally. "And why you're upset."

"Delphians are telepaths?" Nova said to Seth.

Seth shook his head. "Not really. Some of them can... connect with certain species, though. Physically. That adapter on the tank looks interesting."

"Have you come to help?" Celessa said tonelessly.

"What can we do that you can't?" Nova said. "We just came to return your catalyst and to ask about it. It'll kill me unless I keep taking medicine. So I'd like to be rid of it."

"It needs to get to Naiya. They will be able to remove it."

Seth exhaled sharply. "Lovely. It can't be done here?"

"No. It will replicate in Nova's system indefinitely if you remove only some of it. But once you expose a blood vessel to the matrix on Naiya, the catalyst will naturally gravitate to that medium. Like holding a dry sponge to a drop of water." Celessa turned her head slightly toward the Naiyad, listening. "You will return the catalyst to Naiya."

"Oh? Do I hear a 'please' in there?" Nova said.

Celessa opened her eyes. "I think that's more of a question. They sing in their thoughts. She is not easy to understand."

"She? How can you tell it's a she?"

Seth rolled his eyes at Nova. "How did this Naiyad come to be here? Why are you doing this?"

"Last year, before the solstice on Delphi, one of our expeditions found a new keyhole. They should not have entered this new breach, but they did, anyway. They found Naiya, a wonderful world of deep oceans that has no water, no air. Just light and sound and these creatures, these Naiyads, and their sub-species. And water ash, a mere by-product of their oceans and of little value to them. It helps to regulate temperature and certain solar radiation but beyond that it has no purpose."

"Not to them," Seth said.

"Indeed. When our explorers returned they made the grievous error of telling a Union official about their find. The news made its way to your governors. They will obliterate Naiya in their greed for water ash. It is our fault. It is our task to right this wrong."

"And so you developed this catalyst."

"We've done little else since then. We have two other labs working on it. Another was destroyed a while ago. Twice we were able to return to Naiya to bring some of their people with us but now Drackon is guarding the breach. This is the only survivor. We use their... hmm, blood matrix to create the catalyst. She knows that her life is also in peril here."

"So by altering the more valuable water ash properties, you render the planet useless to outsiders," Nova said. "To our own Commonwealth traders and their competitors. We'd suspected that might have been the purpose, but couldn't figure out your motive."

"We tried to reason with them," Celessa said, her hand still on the tank to include the Naiyad in the conversation. "We explained that Naiya's oceans contain sentient life in wonderful variety. Their intelligence rivals that of many of our surface species. But we should know better by now that the ways of your Union are not the ways of Delphi. You need wealth for your wars against the rebel and for things we cannot even fathom."

"Your Clan Council on Delphi was not able to convince them to leave Naiya alone? Maybe even claim Naiya for Delphi?"

"The Council does not know," Celessa said, clearly uncomfortable with this admission. "If they find out about the consequences of our actions they will only use this to further restrict our explorations off-Delphi."

"They would," Seth sighed.

"And we don't lay claim to planets, inhabited or not. So we tried to undo this error by ourselves, far from Delphi. Unfortunately, we have so little understanding of your people that we openly set out to develop the catalyst. Only in these past few months have we learned to hide our laboratories."

"And Drackon has been routing them one by one. To protect the Union's water ash supply." Seth's eyes were on the creature in the tank. Its eerily large eyes studied them with an alien intelligence that seemed to miss nothing. He touched his fingers to the smooth surface of the interface. He longed to spend time in its company, conversing with it the way the Delphian was able to. "How many of them are there on Naiya?"

"Millions."

"And they can't co-exist with outsiders? If this water ash is worthless to them, I mean."

"Did you know Targon once had a native population?

Driven underground now. Bellac used to know peace. As did K'lar Four and Aram. Now they are changed forever by your Union of Commonwealth Planets. Is it any wonder that Delphi strives to keep your people off our shores?" Celessa's cold blue eyes turned to Nova. "You and your Centauri overlords pretend some pointless quest for your primordial ancestors among these worlds, what you call Trans-Targon. But you want more than to find some ancient brothers among us. What can these Naiyads do to withstand your machines and planes and the products of your presence on their world? They do not even carry that genetic fragment you consider so sacred. You will have to see Naiya for yourself to understand what I mean."

They were interrupted when Kiely entered the Naiyad's room. "We've got a positive, Celessa," he said. "The Human's got the catalyst."

"Wonderful!" Celessa said. She leaned toward the creature in the tank and they appeared to exchange some thoughts.

Seth watched the technician leave. "If what you say is correct and the Naiyads can extract the catalyst then all we have to do is take Nova to Naiya?"

"Technically."

"What do you mean?"

"The only way to get to that planet is via an uncharted and still dangerously unstable keyhole. There are no beacons to help you find the way. Can I hope that you are a Level Three spanner?"

Seth shook his head. "I'm just a chartjumper, as is Nova. But the *Dutchman* has a feeder interface." He glanced at Nova. Like his crossdrive upgrade, that interface was cleared for use only on Air Command Eagles.

"You just hope you have the shields to match that, Mister," she said, no longer surprised by his revelations. She turned back to Celessa. "How were *you* going to get the box to Naiya?"

"Our spanner was also on the *Dyona*. He was supposed to

meet that private cruiser on Magra. He is lost to us now and we don't have another."

"A Delphian?"

"Yes, of course."

"I don't think he died up there. The pirates took a few people off the ship before the air went bad. I'm sure one of them was the Delphian we picked up on Pelion. Tall, skinny, long blue hair?"

"You just described half of Delphi's population," Seth pointed out.

"His name was... is Caelyn," Celessa said. "We thought him dead. Lost with the ship. The others will be so relieved to hear that." Her eyes focused on something in the middle distance, as if remembering something. "He... he is very dear to me. Where did they take him?"

"I have no idea."

Celessa's shoulders slumped.

Nova looked up at Seth. "You could find out where they keep him, if he's still alive."

"Nova, I—"

"You can?" Celessa said, sounding hopeful. "How?"

"He's got friends in low places," Nova said and poked a finger into his ribs.

The Delphian lifted a fine blue eyebrow. "Rebels?" She frowned and the Naiyad twisted in its tank in agitation. "Look, if you two are rebels we might have the same goals against the Union but don't draw us into your schemes. We have enough troubles of our own."

Seth raised his hands. "Nothing like that," he said. "We'll head over to Magra and see if we can find out some things. People talk, maybe I can pick up some rumors."

"Please, you must get this catalyst to Naiya. I can't see any other way to save Naiya from your people." Celessa turned her attention to the tank. After some unheard exchange, she removed her hand from the plate and the Naiyad slowly sank from view. "Forgive me. That sounded harsh. And of course you have your own reasons for going there. If you can... If you can find Caelyn and return him safely, I... we would be indebted to you." She gestured to the door. "I'll join you in a moment."

Nova and Seth walked back to the exit of the building to retrieve their pressure suits. She was slow to climb into hers, still awed by Celessa's revelation about the colonel. "Do you think it's really possible?" she said.

"What?" Seth replied, unusually morose. "That nobody gives a damn what happens to the Naiyads or that we can find a misplaced Delphian boyfriend in any one of a dozen rebel holds?"

Nova studied his face, surprised and concerned by his tone. "Yeah, that," she said finally and reached up to lock his collar clamp. "We'll get there, don't you worry."

"Getting there isn't the problem."

Celessa joined them. "I have told the others that there is hope for Caelyn. They are as encouraged and excited as I am. He will be able to communicate with the Naiyads if you get there."

"*When* we get there," Nova said firmly.

Celessa helped them fasten their suits. "I need you to understand how much this means to us. It will be weeks before we have enough of the catalyst to make another attempt to reach Naiya. If we can find another spanner to help us. By that time it may well be too late."

Nova was about to reply when they were interrupted. "Celessa," Kiely leaned into the airlock, "two more ships are coming up this way. Not any of the mining companies. Either your new friends there brought trouble or trouble is coming to meet them. And us."

"Let's go," Seth jammed Nova's helmet over her head. "We can head them off."

"We can get below ground here," Celessa suggested. She looked back into the lab where her colleagues were frantically snatching up display screens and equipment. "This building sits atop some of the mining shafts. If we can move the tank..."

Nova shook her head, knowing that Seth would not leave the *Dutchman* exposed on the surface. She also suspected that, like her, he was eager to inflict a little damage to Drackon's agents by now. "Close the hatch and take cover. Go!"

Celessa nodded and hurried inside. Seth and Nova waited for the room to depressurize and then bounded across the open space between the building and the *Dutchman*, faster than recommended in this gravity. Seth signaled the plane to lower the ramp and they rushed inside, again nervously awaiting pressurization before racing into the cockpit without discarding their suits.

"Get the guns," Seth snapped as he prepared the *Dutchman* for a speedy takeoff.

Nova linked her neural node to the *ship*'s tactical systems and brought them online while Seth prepared for launch. They heard one of the Delphians on the moon calmly ask for identification of the newcomers and then repeat his request a few moments later. There was no reply.

"Two cruisers, no Union markings or signals," Nova reported. "Armed to the eyeballs," she added.

Seth lifted the *Dutchman* from the moon's surface and hovered over the laboratory building. Again, they listened to the Delphian's attempts to contact the ships. It was not long before the real-video screens showed the Fleetfoot class cruisers that, like the *Dutchman*, were used most often as private conveyance or by small transport companies. And rebels.

"I'll wait till they take a shot," Nova said.

"Why? You don't think they're hostile?"

"No, because I think they're Union agents and I am in enough trouble without firing on my own people without provocation."

He grinned. "You're probably right. Not your fault if they don't identify themselves, though."

"Like that nurse back on Targon?"

"Good point."

The two cruisers swooped low over their heads and resolved Nova's quandary by rattling a volley of projectiles off the *Dutchman*'s shields. They continued onward to strafe the metal building on the ground.

Seth rotated the *Dutchman* and raced toward the lead plane at breakneck speed as it came about for another barrage. Nova guided their fire via her neural link, moving seamlessly with Seth's maneuvers until the enemy ship's shields had shredded and her guns impacted their hull. Seth whooped in excitement when the cruiser cartwheeled out of control and smashed into the moon's surface.

"The other one!" Nova yelled. "Where's the other one?"

Seth came about and raced back to the facility. The second cruiser was looping over the buildings, lobbing projectiles into the dusty ground. They saw half-hearted and disorganized laser fire from the direction of the mining ships, still on the ground, as the Delphians' neighbors realized that an assault of some sort was under way. A direct hit from the attack ship slammed into the lab's airlock and destroyed the hatch. Nova cursed and switched to laser fire to drive the cruiser out into space but it swooped around to take another run at the building.

"Missile lock!" Nova shouted when her sensors conveyed the enemy ship's armament configuration. "Gods, Seth, they're going to—"

Too late. Both Seth and Nova gasped when their sensors followed the trajectory of the missile and its terminal impact on the building. Shrapnel spun into the sky, barely slowed by the moon's minimal gravity.

"Bastard." Seth took up pursuit again, this time chasing the cruiser away from the moon. "Kick his ass, Nova."

She blasted her guns into the fleeing ship, more than necessary, and felt little satisfaction when it rolled and fell to pieces under her assault. Seth immediately turned back to Tyra moon.

But there they were greeted with a barrage of laser fire as the few ships belonging to the mining companies aimed their weapons toward the returning *Dutchman*. Nova scanned the location of the Delphians' lab, seeing only a new crater on the moon's surface. "Let's get out of here," she said glumly. "No point in trying to explain who we are."

Seth swung away from Tyra. He punched dispiritedly at the controls to set the autopilot's top speed toward the jumpsite to Magra. They sat in silence for a long while before Nova climbed out of her seat, hampered by the bulky suit she still wore.

"All this just over money, Seth," she said. "There has to be a way to stop these people. *My* people! Not just some grunts overstepping their orders. Colonels! If they can do this over some trade goods, I can't even think about what else they're up to."

He joined her in the main cabin. "Our only proof of any of this just got blown to pieces. We have only your word about what you heard her say about Drackon."

"And yours."

He loosened her neck clamp, his eyes on his hands. "Well, my word doesn't count for much with your people."

She nodded and set to removing the seals on his suit as well. They worked quietly, almost absent-mindedly, lost in their own thoughts until Nova realized the strange intimacy of their task. She looked up at him when her suit dropped to the floor to pool around her feet. He had already stepped out of his and bent to pick them both up when she stopped him.

He looked into her face. "What is it?" he asked, smiling uncertainly. He watched in astonishment as her fingers slipped into the fastener of her shirt and parted it from her neck to below her navel. No other clothing covered the tantalizing glimpse of bare skin she exposed. He recognized the soft look in her deep green eyes although it had been a long time since he had last seen it. "I... I thought you didn't like me anymore," he said thickly.

"But I need you. Now."

He took a step backward, unable to look away. "No, you don't."

She held out her hands. "Don't you want this?"

"Not like this," he breathed, his eyes on her lips. "Not if—"

She touched his chest and moved closer to him. He put his hands on her shoulders, meaning to keep her away. Instead, he watched breathlessly as his fingers pushed her shirt aside until it, too, fell to the floor. He exhaled audibly when she stepped into his arms and tilted her head to brush her lips over his. All reason fled when he bent to kiss her and felt her arms around him, her strong body pressed against his. It was only a few steps to the lounger on which he had slept alone for too many nights.

He was rough, his movements impatient, and his embrace as hard as the lips that crushed hers. Nova responded in kind, seeking the oblivion his tough body offered, even if only for a moment. The awful melancholy both of them had felt since leaving the moon vanished, replaced by the basest of needs that each knew the other could answer. Their bodies met in a violent tempest, leaving both of them exhausted and out of breath when, at last, he collapsed at her side.

"I don't think I've ever seen you sweat before," she grinned.

He pushed his hair out of his face and propped himself on his elbows. "Does this mean we're friends now?"

She stretched and purred and smiled at him. "Does it have to mean something?" she said. "I needed this. And I think you did, too."

His forehead furrowed into a mystified frown. "Is that what this was? A shot in the arm like your meds to keep you functioning?"

"In a way, I suppose."

He sat up and fished through a tangle of clothes at the end of the lounger to find a loose pair of trousers. He slipped into them and paced across the cabin. She watched him check their course before turning back to her. The cold expression on his face startled her.

"Dammit, Nova, why did you do this?"

She sat up but did not bother to cover herself. "Why are you upset..."

"How about you stop using me to get what you need. Is this really so easy for you?"

She frowned. "I did not hold a gun to your head."

"Because you know you don't need to."

She dropped her eyes. "I didn't think it would matter that much to you."

He took a deep breath. "You don't know me at all, then. And I don't understand *you* anymore. You, of all people, fall into bed with a rebel? You'd rather get busy with a damn Rhuwac."

"That is not true! How dare you!"

He turned away. "Put some clothes on."

Only her long waves of hair covered her when she walked to where he stood. "Seth..."

He shook his head. "Leave it alone, Nova. You hate what I've become. What I do. I am nothing to you anymore. If I were anyone else you would have shot me when you had the chance. Don't make things worse by playing games."

She touched his arm. "It doesn't have to be like that," she said. "You don't have to do this."

He pulled out of her grasp. "I can't change what I am any more than you can, Lieutenant."

NINE

"Do you see the pattern, Kada?" The Caspian in the center of the spherical room indicated the illuminated wall with a sweep of his arm.

Seth stepped into the display and closed the door behind him. He remained there but joined Pe Khoja in admiring the view that surrounded them. If not for the floor on which they stood and the gravity that made that possible, both men appeared to float in space, illuminated only by the three-dimensional field of stars. He recognized Trans-Targon, viewed from a distance and showing most of the solar systems within reach of the jumpsites.

"Pattern?" he said. Was the Caspian looking for constellations?

Pe Khoja twisted to look at him briefly before turning his gaze back to the panorama. "Yes, a pattern," he said in unaccented Union mainvoice. "It's there, if you know how to see it." He brushed a six-fingered hand over the wall. It responded to his touch and the image shifted closer to Targon, the planet that represented the center of the Commonwealth in this sector. "See, over here is Delphi." Pe Khoja tapped a solar system to add a red marker to the display. "Just one short jump from Targon. And here, Feyd. There, Magra. And Bellac, K'lar, Pelion and my home, Caspia."

Seth raised his arm to let his hand travel through the hologram. "And you see a pattern there?" he asked, allowing himself to be intrigued by Pe Khoja's musings. It was not often that the Caspian was in a mood to talk but when he did it was worth listening.

"No, because I don't know what I'm looking for. Nor do your people, but it's here. Or maybe out there." He gestured to the opposite side of the sphere displaying distant galaxies. "That one single thing, that one moment that decided to make brothers of us all."

Seth raised an eyebrow. "It's not like you to get philosophical."

The rebel shrugged. "Creation myths don't interest me. Facts do. Like the fact that you, Centauri, and your Humans decided to come all the way out here to meddle in our affairs."

"Well, that's more like you."

"The sooner you are wiped out of this sector, the better. But that's not likely, is it? Three hundred years here in what you named Trans-Targon and you've taken hold like a fungus. You multiply like rodents and you bring more and more of your people here. Conquering and plundering, claiming entire worlds for yourselves in pretended kinship."

"You've done a bit of that yourself," Seth reminded him.

Pe Khoja turned from the display that surrounded them to observe Seth with flat yellow eyes. Seth had to remind himself that he did, indeed, share most of his DNA with this person even though, of the races Pe Khoja had named, the Caspian was the most dissimilar. Unlike the others, his body was covered with short, tawny hair, with a fine pattern of narrow stripes on his head and back. While his hands had two thumbs, his large bare feet were three-toed, calloused and clawed. The golden eyes slanted in a streamlined, elongated face. For all of this, he was as closely related to a

Delphian or a Feydan as Seth himself was. "I don't pretend kinship," he said.

"Your Arawaj followers might be mostly Caspian but half of the rebels recruited for the Shri-Lan are Centauri or Human. Tharron has benefitted from the migration."

"That is true. Bringing together all of the rebel factions to stand against your Union is just a matter of time and patience. Our union against yours."

"Almost poetic."

The Caspian let the display zoom out until it included the distant Centauri binary system. Another tap added a network of well-charted jumpsites that made travel between Trans-Targon and Seth's ancestral home possible. "Someday someone will find a keyhole that will make all of these gates unnecessary. Who knows? Perhaps you will be able to jump the distance in a single span. Isn't that what your explorers hope for?" He marveled at the display. "Perhaps it's always been there. Perhaps that is how we all came to be here, at the same time in our evolution. A single door, out there somewhere, looking only for the right combination of numbers to make it possible. And passable. Surely a miracle."

Seth considered the possibility. A single gateway between the two sectors would change everything. Instead of undertaking a two year journey, twenty billion Centauri and nine billion Humans, would be only a few seconds away from the rich and fertile planets of Trans-Targon. It would not take another three hundred years to bring them here.

"What I fail to understand," Pe Khoja continued. "is why not more people of this sector rise up with Tharron to annihilate your species and take back what is ours. You are a plague."

"With better guns." Seth turned when the door behind him opened. He threw a questioning glance back at Pe Khoja but the Caspian showed no surprise at the intrusion.

"Colonel Drackon," the rebel said. "We were just talking about you. Or, rather, your esteemed kinsmen."

The Human stepped into the room, squinting to make

out their shapes in the dark. His civilian clothes seemed as out of place on him as a uniform would look on Seth. "Not only am I forced to find you inside a damn museum, but you have the nerve to use my name. You are taking a gamble with our good will."

"Your good will is the product of our willingness to do your dirty work. And here you are, asking for more favors."

"Which are well paid for. Who's the Centauri?"

Seth had taken a step back into the deeper shadows, aware that, in this light, his eyes were emitting their identifying glow. He was suddenly glad that he had won his argument with Nova when she had questioned his decision to meet Pe Khoja alone. At the time he had simply wanted to put a safe distance between them for a while. Now it seemed that his intuitions had once again averted disaster. She had been identified on the video taken from the *Dyona* and surely Drackon would recognize her from that. He hoped that the colonel would not recognize him, as well.

"Going to need a pilot to ship those ten thousand lovely flash mods you've brought with you," Pe Khoja said. "Now what is it you're wanting from us this time?"

"I'm looking for two people. Mostly, I want the Delphian your men took off the *Dyona*. Once I have him, you can have the modules. They're here on Magra now."

"I think the modules were a gift to put us in a mood to keep the keyhole coordinates to ourselves, were they not?" Pe Khoja said, appearing to enjoy himself immensely. He searched his memory for a moment. "I'm not sure that we currently have a Delphian in our inventory."

"What do you want for him?" Drackon sounded like his patience needed little more to break completely. Seth almost sympathized with the man. Compromised or not, to have to negotiate with a rebel of Pe Khoja's notoriety would go against every instinct the colonel possessed.

It was rumored that the Caspian was the power behind Tharron's throne now and that the leader relied heavily on Pe Khoja's advice and logistical talents. Where before the

Shri-Lan had acted with brute force to oppose and sabotage the Union, they now showed evidence of organization and planning. Pe Khoja, as remorseless and brutal as most of Tharron's inner circle, used his superior intelligence to organize extortion, black markets and, like now, the subversion of Union members. He rarely dirtied his own hands.

"I'll let him go for a mere one thousand additional modules," he said. "Delivered to our people near Naiya."

Seth was sure that he heard the colonel growl.

"Who's the other one you're looking for?"

"A Human woman also taken off the *Dyona* by your people. Union officer. Whiteside. She showed up on Targon later and then disappeared."

"I don't recall anyone mentioning an officer," Pe Khoja said. "But I'll ask around."

"She doesn't matter as much. I just need her gone, if she's still alive. Where are you holding the Delphian?"

"Certainly not here on Magra. We'll have to deliver him to you." Pe Khoja pointed a thumb at Seth. "He'll take the modules to K'lar and we'll send someone to get the Delphian for you."

"I'm not sure that my ship can carry that much cargo," Seth said quickly. "You can easily get another liftplane for that. I'll deliver the Delphian. My crew cabin's been refitted to house ungrateful company."

Drackon shrugged. "Matters none to me." He glowered at Pe Khoja. "I need you to send him to the station outside the Naiya breach. It's taking our people far too long to chart the jumpsite. Rellius is not a patient man."

Seth had to take a slow and deep breath to hide his astonishment. Rellius? A Factor was pulling the strings here? It was almost too audacious to believe that any of the Union's top level governors would use rebels to achieve their objectives. Or, for that matter, that one of them was willing to wipe out an entire species. His mental image of Nova finding out about this nearly made him grin.

"He's a spanner?" Pe Khoja's short laugh sounded like a bark. "Those Delphians are truly multi-purpose."

"You have the Delphian working for you?" Seth brushed his hair back from his forehead. With luck the illumination in this room was enough to ensure adequate recordings of the colonel and Pe Khoja. He scratched his chin to give the camera in his bracelet another chance to capture the image.

"I'm not sure I would call it that," Pe Khoja said. "But we are keeping him occupied. From what I hear he's not happy with the arrangement."

"Just get him out there," the colonel said. "In shape to do the work. I am heading there myself and will expect you within days. And I'm talking Targon time. Rellius wants that gate fully charted and safe for transit before the next council meeting. I'll have the extra modules with me."

"Yessir, Colonel, sir!" The Caspian saluted and managed to make it look like an insult.

Both Seth and Pe Khoja watched Drackon leave the room without another word.

"He is not a happy man," Seth said. "Been working for him long?"

Pe Khoja's long upper lip lifted in a sneer. "It might be healthier for you to remember that Tharron is the man in charge here, not this Union turncoat or his traitorous overlord. I hope you noticed that I did not mention to him it was you who botched the job on the *Dyona*."

Seth shrugged. "Wasn't my command. Maybe if you'd told them what they were stealing they'd be a bit more careful with the merchandise."

"I've dealt with Gwain. And if you hope to take his place here on Magra you'd better come up with a few success stories to share with Tharron."

"I'll start with your delivery. Where is this Delphi?"

Pe Khoja smirked. "On Aram."

Seth groaned. "Should have guessed you weren't keeping him somewhere pretty."

"You volunteered. Get over there and find Pramman Raj

at Ge'er. He'll dig up that spanner for you. If he's still alive. Pop the officer if you find her there. I don't want to handle uniforms, anyway."

"Where am I taking the Delphi?"

Pe Khoja's hand whipped toward him to grasp his wrist. Seth flinched, ready to evade the Caspian's grasp when he realized that his data sleeve was the object of interest. "Nervous?" Pe Khoja taunted, his yellow eyes glittering in the dark. He accessed Seth's unit to enter the required coordinates for both the Aram location as well as the keyhole to Naiya. Seth forced himself to remain immobile, waiting for Pe Khoja to realize that the leather bracelet next to the array contained a video recorder.

The rebel released his arm. "Like the good colonel said, you're in a hurry." Pe Khoja turned back to his contemplation of the panorama of drifting stars on the curved walls. "Before I forget, Centauri..." he said as Seth headed for the door.

Seth waited.

"You wouldn't know anything about Comori's lab on Aikhor suffering an extreme collapse, would you?"

"Not a thing."

"You were there. Seen with a Bellac whore. Your ship was serviced, too. Does that help you to remember?"

Seth smiled carelessly, wondering how Pe Khoja managed to know the things he did. "Yes, she was sweet."

"There were some valuable goods in that lab, Kada. It takes a lot of currency to maintain a ship like yours." His flat eyes narrowed as he scrutinized the Centauri. "I will not have you playing your own games at Tharron's expense. That'll just get you dead. Am I clear there?"

"Anything else?"

The Caspian waved his hand to dismiss him from this meeting. "Step carefully, Kada. Don't be more trouble than you're worth."

* * *

Nova's attention was only partially captivated by the furred little animal in her lap batting at a string dangling from her wide-brimmed hat. Vincent had insisted that the pilot visiting his home received a good dose of sunshine and fresh air before heading back into the doubtlessly damaging environment of filtered gas and artificial gravity she called home at any other time. He was probably right, Nova thought, inhaling the fragrant air here in this garden, perceiving scents she had not experienced before. More of her attention was diverted by a large insect buzzing around her head, probably fully equipped with various stingers and blood-sucking proboscises.

But for the most part her thoughts were on Seth and the awkward and cold atmosphere that had settled over the *Dutchman* ever since their disturbing encounter after leaving Pelion two days ago. There had been no more jokes at her expense, no more teasing or lewd remarks. Their conversation was polite and limited to the operations of the ship and their plans for coming here to Magra.

Upon arrival, he had dropped her off at Vincent's cottage and had gone on his own to seek out his contacts while Acie and Nova took a skimmer into the nearby city to pick up Nova's medicine. He had been gone for a few days now, and she worried.

Nova regretted her impulsive seduction of Seth aboard the *Dutchman*, wondering if she had hurt him, surprised that he could be hurt. But he had left her without a word six years ago - surely she had not meant much to him then. And now they were on opposite sides of an armed conflict growing increasingly violent between the Union and Tharron's rebel organizations. On opposite sides, yet each day that passed increased his significance, drew her closer to people like Acie and Vincent, and led her to question her unwavering loyalty to the Union's Air Command.

She stared moodily at her arm, abused by days of injections. If not for their mission to save her life as well as the Naiyads', she should be long gone, returned to the strict confines of military life, unthinking and unquestioning as before.

It was not too late. The nearest Air Command base was only a continent away, within easy calling distance. Even a skimmer could get her there in a few days. But whom could she trust? Colonel Carras' motives were unclear and she had to admit that she felt compelled to believe Celessa's accusations against Colonel Drackon. Her own CO and likely her father, too, would just direct her back to Targon to report all of this. To Carras.

"Nova!" she heard Acie's bright voice. "Seth's back. And Vincent made dumplings."

Nova rose out of the lounger. Acie, as usual, wore an oversized lab coat and her white hair hung in several messy braids. She hadn't told Nova what she was working on in her basement lab and Nova didn't want to know. She fussed with the ball of fur that insisted on climbing up her arm. Didn't looking the other way when every bit of her training compelled her to investigate make her a collaborator? Had she learned nothing on Bellac, less than a year ago?

"What's wrong?" Acie's smile wavered.

Nova inhaled deeply of the sweet air breezing through the garden and gave the woman a quick smile. "All's well," she lied and hooked her arm around Acie's waist.

They entered the kitchen at nearly the same moment that Seth came into the room from the front of the cottage. "I have great news, Vincent," he proclaimed. "You are going to congratulate me only moments from now." He halted abruptly when he nearly collided with Nova at the back door. His smile faded and he stepped away. Acie's brows drew together in a puzzled frown when she looked from Seth to Nova and back again.

Vincent turned from his stove, wiping his hands. "Great news is always welcome."

Seth went to a side board and fetched a display screen. He placed it on the table in the middle of the room like a magician about to perform a trick. The others came closer when he downloaded something from his bracelet to the monitor. "Watch this."

They looked at the screen, disoriented by the poor lighting in the planetarium and the movements of Seth's wrist unit.

"Who's that?" Acie wanted to know.

Seth froze the display. "Pe Khoja, Tharron's best pal."

She cocked her head in appraisal. "He's handsome." She looked up to see the others staring at her in speechless astonishment. "What? He is!"

"He's the murdering mastermind of your own people's misery," Vincent said. "You'll want to stay far, far out of his way."

She looked back at the screen with a pout. "Why are all the pretty ones such bastards?"

"Thanks," Seth said. He restarted the video. "Can we continue?"

They returned their attention to the screen to watch the meeting between Pe Khoja, Drackon and Seth, their eyes growing bigger with every moment that passed. Nova gasped when the colonel mentioned the Factor's name. "No! Rellius? Using rebels?"

Seth nodded. "Efficient, huh?"

She watched without further interruption until the recording ended. The video was blurred and at times obscured in the dim light of the exhibit, but both Pe Khoja and Colonel Drackon were clearly recognizable in several of the segments.

Nova sat down, stunned. "Unbelievable."

Vincent chuckled. "This is almost funny. I do hope you don't intend to carry out Pe Khoja's directive to harm our Nova, are you?" He put an arm around her shoulder and gave her a brief squeeze. "After all, the Lieutenant has shown remarkable restraint in your case."

Nova felt her face grow hot and did not dare to look at Seth.

"Wouldn't dream of it," Seth said. He pushed the display

tablet toward her side of the table. "Download this to your system." He pointed at her data sleeve, purchased on her recent trip up the coast with Acie. "And we'll keep a copy on the *Dutchman*. This information is priceless."

"What will you do with it?" she said.

"Nothing. It's what *you* will do with it that is the question here." He shrugged. "I'm just in this to save the squid. And now we know where the Delphian spanner is. Not a bad day's work. We'll have to get more weather gear and an outdoor suit for the Delphian, extra long. Now what is it I'm smelling, Vincent? Did you go and shoot Nova's daram to make that?"

Nova tapped the copy instructions dispiritedly into her wrist unit. She looked up when she felt Acie's eyes on her. "What?"

Acie glanced over at Seth, who was admiring Vincent's culinary creation, and then back to Nova. "What's going on?" she whispered.

Nova shrugged and returned to her task. "Not a thing."

TEN

This time, neither Seth nor Nova relied on the other's help to climb into their outdoor gear before leaving the ship. They layered shirts and trousers and covered them with vests, leggings, padded overcoats and lined boots. A thick burnoose and goggles protected their faces from Aram's extreme temperatures.

"Is it safe to leave the *Dutchman* here?" Nova peered at the real-vid screens showing their surroundings. They had landed without challenge near Ge'er, a scattering of hovels huddled on the edge of a barren plateau lined with massive cliffs. There was not enough surface water for anything more than wispy drifts of snow but their scanners told of deadly temperatures outside. The few people moving among the buildings bundled in thick layers or even heated pressure suits and only the natives, their bodies covered with hair as dense as fur, seemed indifferent to the weather.

"As safe as any place on this rock," Seth replied. He looked over her shoulder at the screen. "I think the tunnel entrance is in that blue building. The actual rebel base is dug into the cliff to the south. Mostly old mine shafts."

"Why would anyone want to live in this place?"

He cinched his overcoat with a gun belt. "Pack a few percussion charges. This place used to do fine business before the last of the crystal was mined. It's not so bad below ground. Maybe not a great place for outsiders, but some of the subsurface habitats are really quite nice. Not this one, though. Not sure I'd even call it a habitat."

"You've been here before?"

He ran his fingers over the scar on his forehead. "Locked up for a few weeks. I may have annoyed the wrong people. It happens."

"This is a prison?"

"Tharron's version of it, yes. It's a place for people to disappear. Or for safe storage. The Delphian might not be in terrific shape, but he's not been here for very long so there's hope."

"Maybe some of the other people from the *Dyona* are here."

He had bent to tie his boots but now looked up, concerned. "Don't lose sight of the job, Nova. Unless the others had value beyond saleable goods, they would not be kept here. Don't make trouble. You're off duty, remember?"

"I can't walk away if they're holding prisoners."

"You can and you will. Those prisoners are mostly rebels, anyway. The bad kind even Tharron doesn't want around. You don't care much for those, if I recall."

She pinched her lips together before some unfortunate retort passed them.

They exited the *Dutchman* and were immediately buffeted by a strong wind cutting through their layers as if they weren't there. Nova stomped her feet to drive away the biting cold while Seth secured the ship and then hurried ahead of him to the structure he had pointed out.

Nova's teeth were chattering when they burst into the building and slammed the door behind them. The ripe curse that escaped her formed a cloud of breath in the air; the interior of the shack was only a few degrees warmer than the outside.

Rough laughter greeted this. Nova removed her goggles and burnoose to get a clearer view of one of the short, dense Aramese natives and two Centauri slouching around a heater, sharing a bottle of something while they waited for their visitors. "Girl is the delicate sort," one of the men said, standing up. "Too cold for you here? Need some warming up?" He reached experimentally for the hem of her jacket.

Nova's gun was pressing against his throat before he had finished the sentence. "Touch that and you never touch anything again."

"Better not irk the lady," Seth said, watching the Centauri take a step back again, assured that Nova would not be taken lightly. "Where's Pramman?"

The rebel scowled at them, chafing under the mocking grins of his companions. "Below. Said to take you down when you got here."

"Then how about you do that?"

The Aramese gestured for them to follow into the rear of the building where a trolley sat on a track of questionable workmanship. He took a seat near the front where the only mechanism seemed to be a brake handle designed to prevent the planet's gravity from hurtling the cart into the depths at terminal velocity. Neither Nova nor Seth felt especially confident when they climbed into the vehicle.

Their journey commenced at a reasonable speed along a narrow tunnel dug into the side of the canyon. The walls were close enough to touch and Nova kept her hands clasped in her lap. The cart jolted around a sharp turn and then the track began to angle downward, snaking its way along a cave system that ranged from vast halls to rough-hewn passages. Nova was reminded of her trip through Targon's bowels and wished for some of the bundles of laundry to cushion this one, as well.

By the time the trolley came to a halt in a shadow-filled cavern her stomach seemed to have turned a few degrees and she closed her eyes for a moment. At least it was warmer down here.

Seth nudged her with his elbow. "That's Pramman over there. Watch your step around that one. He's a tiny man but he'll cut you before you see the knife coming."

"Can't I just shoot him?"

He blinked and turned to her, about to say something, when he realized that she was joking. He gave her what felt like the first real smile in days.

"What's that smell down here?" She wrinkled her nose as they climbed out of the trolley and walked to where the Human waited for them.

"Bad air and Rhuwacs," he said. "Lots of them."

"Rhuwacs? Down here? And you couldn't mention that earlier?"

"They're all right as long as you don't try to pet them."

They came to halt by a metal door set into the stone wall. Pramman inspected them silently, most of his glower directed at Seth. The whites of his eyes shone brightly in his dark face. "Takes guts to show yourself here again, Kada," he said in a surprisingly melodious voice. "If you weren't here on Pe Khoja's orders I'd have you chopped up and fed to the lizards by now. You and your friend."

"Those are harsh words," Seth said. He half turned to Nova. "Prammy and I are old friends."

Pramman turned to unlock the metal door, moving awkwardly as he did so with a hand that was badly mangled and missing several fingers. "It's because of you I'm stuck in this hellhole, Centauri. Never did learn to shoot with my other hand. So now I'm a fucking gatekeeper." He waited for them to step through the door. "You'll pay for that someday."

"Are you going to get our prisoner or just throw idle threats around?" Nova said. "Pe Khoja's waiting."

"Your girlfriend needs to learn manners, Kada," he said without taking his eyes off Nova. She saw that his teeth had been filed to points.

"My *girlfriend* knows who's paying your rent, Pramman. Where is the Delphian?"

The jailer turned and walked through a narrow passageway. Widely spaced lamps along the damp walls offered just enough light to show the hazards of the uneven ground. "With the slaves."

Nova frowned. "You hold slaves here? I thought this was a prison."

Pramman laughter was an unpleasantly staccato giggle. "Do you think you can get anyone to actually work in this place? Voluntarily? Where did you find this child, Kada?" He leered at her. "They're mostly women. For the guards. And for some of the prisoners."

Nova saw Seth wince and felt her own stomach lurch at the thought. But what had she expected in a place like this? She gritted her teeth and did not let her disgust show on her face.

"They tend to get damaged. The Delphi's pretty good at fixing them up again. We'll miss that around here." Pramman stopped to unlock another door. All of them looked around themselves when an eerie howl traveled through the stone passages, echoing for a long time before falling silent again.

"Is that what I think it was?" Nova whispered.

"If you thought that was a Rhuwac shouting for his dinner, you'd be right."

"Sounded like it was dying."

"Possibly."

Nova shuddered. She had seen Rhuwacs on a few occasions, usually from a safe distance. Brutal and without empathy, the massive, lumbering brutes were easily trained to obey the orders of their handlers. Most were capable of rudimentary language skills and some even bore arms. Barely sentient, these creatures were used like foot soldiers by Tharron and often as little more than cannon fodder in ground battles. Massive jaws and upper bodies gave them monstrous proportions. This, combined with unevenly tufted and often cracked, scaled-looking skin invariably instilled terror in anyone unfortunate enough to encounter them. Many of Nova's squad mates called them 'target practice' when from the safety of a fighter plane but in close combat they were nothing less than tanks.

"They're bred here, trained here. This is just one of a few places where this happens," Seth said. "Hard to find places that'll let you keep this sort of zoo."

"True," Pramman said. "We're overcrowded here with almost three hundred of them. But they're being shipped off to the Mrak sector soon. They're running a bit low over there and I hear Pe Khoja has something special planned for Mrak Four." He giggled again, unaware of Nova's raised eyebrows as she made a mental note of that information. He pulled on the heavy door which opened faster when Seth pitched in. "Here you are. Your Delphi is in there somewhere. Come knocking back here if you find him."

Nova and Seth walked through the crude doorway and into a subterranean cavern. The gate slammed behind them, the sound echoing from one massive cave wall to another for a while. Vague light sources along the jagged walls glinted along veins of crystal, the remnants of the mother lode around which this mine had been built. They stepped carefully around boulders and stalagmites and then crossed a stagnant water channel via metal plates placed across it. Something dripping somewhere nearby was the only sound.

"Spooky." Nova drew her gun and peered into an empty antechamber. "Where is everybody?"

"Hello?" Seth called out, his gun also in his hand. "Shan Caelyn?"

Nova spun when another howl rang through the corridors outside. It was a haunting, tormented noise that cut through to her bones. "I don't think I've ever wanted to get out of a place as badly as this one."

"That makes two of us," a voice to their left made itself heard.

A tall, lanky shape emerged from the shadows and stepped over a boulder toward them. The man's clothes were torn and stained but his tranquil expression did not reflect the hardships of his captivity. His face was clean and the blue hair hung in a neat braid over his shoulder. When Nova looked past him she saw a few ragged prisoners, mostly females, stare at them suspiciously from the recesses of the cave.

The Delphian stopped to observe the new arrivals for a few moments, his hands clasped serenely behind his back. "I've seen you before," he said to Nova with the clipped accent common among his people. "You were on our ship. One of the guards." His gaze shifted to Seth. "And you were with the pirates. And now you're brought down here by that rebel jailer. I'm not sure that I quite know what to make of you."

"Well, it's all very complicated," Nova said. "But we've come to get you out. Shan Celessa sent us. Come quickly."

The dark blue of the Delphian's eyes brightened at the mention of that name. "How is my Elder Sister?"

"Time for that later," Nova said. "We have to go."

"No, I cannot," he said. He turned to gesture at the captives now cautiously drawing closer. There were Humans among them and also Centauri and a few Bellac. All of them gaunt and pale, dressed in cheap one-piece suits and layers of rags against the cold. "I'm needed here. I have a little healing ability. Their lives are terrible."

"Delphians!" Seth sighed. "You're also needed on Naiya."

"That is true." Caelyn seemed to ponder this for a moment. "Then we must take them with us. Some of them are sick and will not recover in this place."

Seth lowered his voice. "We can't take them. We don't have the means to do that. Or a ship large enough. We can send for help, perhaps."

"I've already tried," Caelyn said. "That Bellac woman over there, Kala, stole a data unit that I was able to reset to send a transmission some days ago. No one came. I thought perhaps you had come to answer my call. But I suppose no one heard it, after all."

"That is likely. You are far underground here," Nova said.

"Don't underestimate a Delphian's ability to tamper with

your simple technology. As long as you can find the correct frequency, these walls still hold enough crystal for amplification."

"Really?" Seth said, interested. He looked up at the cave ceiling to see the veins of crystal glittering in the fitful light of their lamps. "What power source did you use?"

Nova cuffed his arm. "Can we leave the science to the Delphian and get back to this?"

The woman Caelyn had pointed out earlier stepped closer to them. "There is another way out, but it's through the Rhuwac holds. It leads to shipping doors at the base of the cliff. They used to take ore out that way, before this place was made into a prison."

Nova looked to Seth. "That could work."

"Nova, we don't have room for them all on the *Dutchman*! Or air."

She pursed her lips. "Is there no safe place nearby? Some town? Other caves?"

The woman shook her head. "None I know of that won't have you frozen to death before you reach them. We barely have enough to keep us warm down here."

Nova frowned. "Can't stay, can't leave. Ridiculous. I'm a Union officer and I will be able to reach someone at Air Command. We'll take Caelyn back out with us, as planned. Once we're off planet I'll advise Air Command about this place and that you're trapped down here. They'll want to know about the Rhuwacs as well. It won't be long before they get here."

There were a few hesitant nods and, finally, one from Caelyn. "How soon do you think—"

"Do you hear that?" one of the women standing a little apart from the others said, sounding frightened.

"What?" Seth said, listening for whatever it was that had startled her.

Voices echoed through the corridors, some of them shouting. Distantly a few explosions reverberated through the stone. Nova and Seth exchanged a worried glance, familiar with the sounds of battle. More shouting, louder now, reached their ears and they hurried to the door.

Nova blasted the lock and kicked at it until the door sprang open. Seth handed a pistol to Caelyn. "Does anyone here know how to use a gun?"

His question was met by wide-eyed bewilderment from the already traumatized prisoners. Then Caelyn shook his head and handed the weapon back to Seth. "I'm a navigator. There are not a lot of warriors among my people."

Just then Pramman rushed toward them. "Union soldiers. On the ground. And with air power. They're at the west exits and we're cut off from the tunnel to Ge'er as well. They are blasting everything. Some of the shafts are filling with gas."

"They're incinerating the Rhuwacs?" Caelyn gasped.

"Who cares about the damn lizards! They're going to incinerate everyone else, too!"

"Caelyn, where is that transmitter you said you had?" Seth snapped.

"Transmitter?" Pramman exclaimed. "You have a transmitter? You brought this hell upon us, Delphi?"

Nova's eyes narrowed. "I am really, *really* tired of you." She raised her gun and shot him squarely in the chest. The blast threw him backward, out into the hall. Some of the women shrieked.

Seth looked at the crumpled heap. "I suppose you've been wanting to shoot a rebel for days."

"Does everything have to be so violent with you Union people?" Caelyn said. He reached under his ragged vest to pull out a thin tablet. "No wonder Delphi prefers to keep you away from our planet."

"Wasn't even set to kill," Nova muttered and changed the setting on her gun.

Seth took the transmitter and then pulled the data sleeve form his forearm. "Nova, I may be able to boost a signal using the *Dutchman* from here. Then you better try to call off your dogs before this place comes down on our heads."

She nodded and went out into the hall to listen to the

commotion in the upper levels of the prison. Shouting, the sound of projectile weapons, but all of it still distant. Seth and Caelyn conferred quietly over the transmitter while she paced, a gun in either hand. "You," she gestured at the women. "Collect whatever you have here for clothes and blankets in case you have to go outside. It's damn cold out there. Hurry."

The prisoners scattered to follow her order, new hope on their smudged faces.

"I think this is going to work," Seth said. He handed the unit to Nova. "Make it good, Lieutenant."

She removed a glove and tapped her service number into the transmitter. "Air Command, this is First Lieutenant Nova Whiteside, UAC unit 483. Come in." She waited for a few seconds before trying again. "Do you read? Lieutenant Nova Whiteside calling anybody. I am trapped in the lower holds of the rebel prison south of Ge'er along with just under twenty civilians. Hold your fire."

There was some static. And finally a voice. "Do you read that, Vanguard Twelve?"

"Roger, V6. Awaiting verification."

"What the hell verification do you need? Stop shooting at us! Stand down!"

"Uh, V12, Whiteside currently listed AWOL."

"Yes, that's me," Nova said. "Just stand down!"

The entire cave system seemed to shake as a massive explosion rocked the upper halls. Frightened screams from the prisoners mingled with the sound of rocks falling nearby. Dust showered from the cave ceiling.

"Idiots," Seth said. "Come on, we'll take our chances with the Rhuwacs. Is everyone here now? Kala, lead the way. Stay together."

"Vanguard," Nova tried again. "Come in, dammit. Hold your fire."

Static. Then: "That's a negative, Whiteside. Endeavor to clear civilians from the combat area or take cover. Stand clear."

Seth took the transmitter from her hands and tossed it back to Caelyn. "Give it up, Nova. We're on our own." Another explosion rumbled through the tunnels.

The group hurried to the intersection leading to the slavehold, turning away from the commotion audible from the upper levels to head into the opposite direction. Their progress was painfully slow and the captives slipped and stumbled, bruised themselves on the jagged walls, and cowered in fear with each distant thunder of explosives. It was some time before the crudely chiseled corridors widened and then opened into a larger chamber.

The two Human guards were too surprised by the arrival of an untidy rabble of prisoners to do much but come to their feet. Seth strode across the room, grasped one of them by the throat and slammed him against the wall. He raised the gun in his other hand and shot his companion. "Is that clear to you?" he said to the man on the wall.

"Wha... what's going on? Who... what—"

Seth jammed the gun under the man's nose. "Clear to you?"

"Yes!"

"Whoa," Nova said softly when she discovered the bizarre collection of tools kept here. Storage hooks and bins displayed chains, leather harnesses, cudgels, stun guns, hoods and blinds and whips, the tools of the trade for the guards and handlers of Rhuwacs. "Creepy."

"Take a look, Red." Seth jerked his chin toward a door opposite of the one through which they had entered.

She peered into a long hallway lined by walls made of metal bars. Hulking shapes moved behind them and she heard grunts and murmurs and occasional snarls. Some of the Rhuwacs slouched on two-tiered bunks, others paced aimlessly or huddled in small groups on the floor. Their rough-spun cloaks and kilts were as ragged as those of the prisoners. A light blinked beside a metal double-door at the end of the central walkway. It seemed very far away.

She walked over to the handler still pinned to the wall. "Is that door keyed to your hand?"

"Yes," he grunted, barely able to breathe. His hands were wrapped around Seth's forearm but he did not struggle.

"Does it lead outside?"

"Not that door. But the ones beyond, yes."

"Union coming this way, so your only way out is with us. Going to play nice?"

"Yes!"

Seth released him. "Where does the exit lead to?"

The man rubbed his bruised neck. "Base of the cliff," he said angrily. "Used to be a shipping area for crystal."

"Any air cars there?"

"Maybe one or two. Not enough for everyone. Soon be too cold to go out that way, anyhow."

Seth turned to the others. "Grab some of those cloaks. They probably stink but it's better than freezing to death." He looked through the door into the Rhuwac hold. "Cazun strike me, what a mess," he whispered.

"Not much choice," Nova said as they listened to more explosions in the distance.

"At least they're locked up. Probably haven't been trained much yet to be out on their own." He looked over to their handler. "Those cages *are* locked, I'm assuming?"

"Yeah. These are mean ones. Culled out because they're untrainable. You don't want to get close to the bars."

Caelyn stood nearby, examining a collar spiked with metal prongs. "You use this on those people?" he said to the handler.

"Only thing that keeps 'em from tearing your throat out, yeah. Fucking animals."

"Animals? Those are sentient beings. Your Union declared them thus!"

Nova put a hand on his arm and took the collar away. "Not all of them can... understand our ways, Caelyn. They are dangerous."

"If you make them so. Torture them with these. Lock them in cages in the dark." He shook his head, bemused.

"What a strange world I've stumbled into."

"I won't argue that," Seth said. He raised his voice so that the others heard. "The guard, Kala, you two and Caelyn go first, then the rest of you. Everyone just stay to the center of the hall and move as fast as you can. Nova and I will bring up the rear. You'll see about fifty or so Rhuwacs behind bars on both sides. They'll start making a colossal racket. Just keep going. Stay away from the walls, do not turn, don't even look at them."

There were uncertain nods all around.

"Shan Caelyn, if this rebel decides to change his mind, give him one of your Delphian brain bolts."

Caelyn raised both eyebrows, baffled. "Ah, yes," he said. "Brain bolt. Very painful." He glanced at Nova with a secret smile in his bright blue eyes when the handler took a hasty step away from him.

Seth opened the entrance to the Rhuwac hold. "Go. Quick!"

The prisoners stepped into the hall, not without cries of terror when the Rhuwacs spotted them and began to rush the cage walls. Nova winced when she saw scaled arms thrust through the bars toward the terrified women. The central walkway was barely wide enough to stay out of their reach. Hoarse shouts and curses rose in volume as they grew more excited. Double rows of tombstone teeth were bared and blunt fists beat against the bars that suddenly seemed awfully flimsy.

"Don't look at them," she yelled. "Run. Go go go!"

A high-pitched scream rose above the noise when one of the women stumbled and fell to the stone floor, crying out in terror when a massive hand grasped her leg. Caelyn kicked at the arm and stomped onto the thick wrist until the Rhuwac released its prey and he was able to pull her to her feet again. Another of the beasts swung a fist at him and he took a sharp blow to the chest before leaping out of the way. The noise made by the enraged Rhuwacs was deafening.

"Keep going," Seth shouted.

Nova watched the handler, more experienced than any of them with these creatures, reel in terror past the cages. They turned their furor upon him, shouting his name along with other words that made little sense to any of them. Panicked, he collided with a prisoner and then slammed into one of the cage doors.

"Watch out!" Nova shouted but one of the brutes reached around the man's neck and pulled him toward the cage. The Human screeched in terror when the arm tightened and his head was forced between the bars of the enclosure. She froze when the Rhuwac bit the side of his face.

A row of pulsating red lights came on above the cell doors. "Now what?" Seth gasped at the same time that realization struck him. "They are releasing the Rhuwacs!"

Nova tore her eyes away from the wildly flailing rebel. "What do you—"

"To fight the soldiers. They are letting the Rhuwacs loose down here!" He waved to the women. "Go! Run. Find something to get that door down."

Nova turned back to the handler. His movements were weakening in the Rhuwac's grip and the side of his head was an unrecognizable pulp of flesh and bone. She shot first him, then the monster clawing at him. She was only dimly aware of Seth shouting her name when she took the man's wrist and pressed her gun to his elbow. The charge shattered the joint and anything else keeping his forearm attached to his body. She turned and ran after Seth, hearing the metal squeal of the cell doors opening on either side of her.

Well-placed fire from Seth's weapons streaked past her to hold back the furious Rhuwacs pouring into the central walkway. The lumbering bodies were built for strength, not speed, but she felt one of them grasp the back of her coat. Before he was able to jerk her off her feet Seth had hit his mark and the Rhuwac fell, slowing those that followed.

Nova sprinted the rest of the way to reach the others trapped between the locked door and the horde of Rhuwacs lurching toward them. They leaped out of the way when she got there, holding the severed arm aloft like a gruesome trophy. She slapped it at the door's key pad and punched the release button again and again until the lock disengaged. Caelyn pushed forward to help her slide the door wide enough for the others to get through.

Seth was the last to escape the Rhuwac hold, flinging himself through the door and rolling out of the way when Caelyn and two of the women slammed it shut. A heavy bar was readily in place, no doubt designed to prevent a mass escape of Rhuwacs like the one they had just witnessed.

They waited breathlessly for the Rhuwacs to hurl themselves at the door. It shuddered under the assault of the beasts and strained against its brace but it held. Gradually, the pounding and the furious roars abated. Now that their quarry was out of sight, the Rhuwacs seemed to lose interest.

Both Nova and Seth sprawled on the floor, gasping for breath until the adrenaline surging through their bodies subsided. She realized that she was still holding the dripping arm and hastily tossed it aside before peeling off her blood-soaked gloves.

Seth lurched to his feet and reached down to help her up. "Utterly awesome, Red," he said, shaking his head, grinning. Like her, he had to fight an urge to laugh out loud, knowing that the escapees in the room would think them both quite mad. "Everyone okay?"

"Everyone accounted for, anyway," Caelyn said, looking worriedly at the shell-shocked captives. He reached under his vest and retrieved the improvised transmitter, its casing shattered. "This broke when I got hit. Better that than my ribs, I suppose."

They looked around the mostly empty chamber, likely a loading area carved out of the rock. A trolley stood near a stack of metal pipes and several pallets of cage walls awaited assembly. The massive hinged door led outside, evidenced by the daylight slanting through transom windows above. It also made the room bitterly cold.

"We must be somewhere near the bottom of the cliff."

"And a long way from Ge'er and the *Dutchman*," Nova said.

Seth spun around when someone entered from his right. A baffled-looking Centauri rebel, likely still unaware that Union soldiers were invading the compound, froze in mid-step. Nova took him out before he had a chance to raise an alarm.

"Stay here. Stay quiet," she hissed at the others although by now the raw sounds echoing through the halls would have alerted any other guards that something very strange was going on. She joined Seth on a reconnaissance along the short corridor leading away from the loading dock. An open door led into a break room for the guards. Attempts had been made here to create a more comfortable environment and the walls were clad in molded plastic panels. A video display blared some sort of entertainment segment and Seth shut it off. There was no food here except for some scrapings on a dirty platter. A similar room beside this one appeared to be storage. Nova was happy to see that it contained new bales of the fabric used to clothe the Rhuwacs. They moved on and came to a large hall holding little more than building supplies and fuel tanks.

"No one else down here," Seth reported when they returned to the others. He gestured to Caelyn and the two men moved a few crates to allow access to the transom window above the bay door. "We're in luck." He jumped back down. "Couple of skimmers out there, like the guard said."

Nova glanced at the door to the Rhuwac cells when a guttural scream echoed through the stone chambers. "We're pretty much trapped here for now. It'll be hours before those soldiers clean out the Rhuwacs. There'll be hundreds of them on the loose now."

"Sure sounds like it."

"It's going to be dark shortly and the temperature outside will drop too far for us to leave that way, even by skimmer."

"Yes, we're stuck here for a while, Miss Optimist," Seth said, softening his rebuke with a smile. He addressed the rest of the group. "Listen, everybody. Caelyn, Nova and I will try to make it back to the *Dutchman* at first light. We'll make sure the Union soldiers know you're back here. You will be fine here until then. Just don't open that door." He considered a moment. "If by mid-day it doesn't look like we made it, some of you will take the other skimmer and try to locate a Union patrol. Make sure you know they're uniforms. Any left-over rebel will take your car and leave you walking out there."

"Now who's the optimist," Nova grumbled, unheard.

"Why can't you stay here with us till the soldiers come?" one of the women asked.

Seth glanced at Nova. "Well, to be honest, we're wanted elsewhere and Air Command will only slow us down. We'd rather just stay out of their way."

"You are rebels, then?" Caelyn asked. "Just so I know what I've gotten myself into."

"Not today," Nova said tersely. "There are blankets in that storage room and the area beyond there is warmer. There is a tap in there, so at least we have water. See if you can find some containers to fill up in case we lose power. Let's try to get a little rest and stay warm."

The group moved into the hallway where they picked up stacks of the rough material from the storage room and from there settled into a corner of the back hall. There were startled cries when, true to Nova's prediction, the overhead lights dimmed dramatically and several backup units came on when the main power supply to the compound was cut.

Nova thought about the Rhuwacs roaming the lightless tunnels of the prison and shuddered visibly. A Rhuwac's sense of smell would find a Union soldier far sooner than any night vision eyepieces they might carry.

"How are you holding up?" Seth asked, noting her pallor even in the dimmed, orange-tinted light of the emergency lamps.

Nova handed a few more cloaks to the last of the women in the hall and then sat down on the remaining stacks in the storage room. She looked up at him. "You realize they've probably blown the *Dutchman* to bits? I didn't want to mention that out there."

"It's a long way from here. And there are civilians in Ge'er. They won't risk an air strike over the town. And, short of that, they can't really harm the ship."

"They can wait for us to return there."

"Yes, they probably will." He closed the door to the hall against the icy draft and came to sit beside her. "Alternate plan, Nova. If we get captured by Air Command, you and Caelyn will have to convince your mighty leaders in some other way to avoid damage to Naiya. You may have to spend the rest of your life jamming needles into your arm. It's not the end."

"Could be for you."

He shrugged. "Still less painful than being caught by Rhuwacs. And you will still have evidence against Drackon and Rellius. That's worth something."

She flinched when, distantly, a hoarse scream ended in a high-pitched shriek, abruptly cut off. "I think they're turning on each other," she said. "Probably hungry."

"They're not cannibals."

"There are other prisoners. You saw that... thing bite that man."

He grimaced.

"Why did they not stop, Seth?" she said, aware of the hopeless tone in her voice and unable to change it. "Why didn't they damn well stand down when I was recognized? Those were Union pilots. Not just any pilots. Vanguard. But they went ahead anyway, knowing we had civilians down here."

He put a hand on her arm. "Do the math, Nova. What's a handful of civilians compared to a whole nest of rebels and a Rhuwac training camp? Who knows what else Tharron is hiding in this maze? You're collateral damage. This isn't news to you."

"Well, I don't want any more part of this." She covered her ears with her hands when yet another howl tore through the dark. One of the women in the other room cried out in fear. "This is hell, I'm sure of it. I'm cold and tired and hungry. And there are monsters out there in the dark and worse monsters flying over our heads dropping bombs into mine shafts."

Seth put an arm around her shoulders. "Come on, Red, you've seen worse than this. We're safe here. Don't quit on me now."

"What I'm quitting is this damn army," she said. "I've had it. I finally get out of Bellac and where do I end up? In this stinking Rhuwac pit. With my own people shooting at us. I can't do this anymore. And don't act like collateral damage means nothing to you. If it did you wouldn't be risking your neck over a bunch of prisoners."

He picked up one of the cloaks to wrap around her. "I'm risking my neck for *you*," he said after a while, still fussing with the blanket. "You just happen to be a package deal with a couple of million squid, a Delphian and a dozen pleasure slaves."

She looked up at him, wordless.

"You know," he said. "My people don't have your concept of hell, but if this is hell there isn't anyone with whom I'd rather be caught in it."

"You mean that?"

"Yeah, I mean that." His smile was a sad one. "For all it's worth now."

She watched her hand reach up to brush a strand of hair from his eyes. He closed them when she stroked her fingers across his cheek. "It's worth a lot," she said after a while. "No one's ever done what you have for me. And I treat you like..."

"A rebel?"

"Yeah," she said, a trembling smile on her lips. "But I don't care anymore. You are not like them, I know that. I've always known that. I have no right to think anything I do is better than the choices you've made. I'm sorry. I don't—"

He leaned over to touch his lips to hers, stopping her words with a soft, undemanding kiss. "You don't have to apologize," he said. He kissed her again, moving slowly and gently as if they had never kissed before. He took a deep breath. "I've always loved you, you know. I suppose I always will."

This time he did not object when she pulled him down to stretch out beside her on the bales of cloth. She opened her coat and then his and slipped her arms around him to feel his warmth and share her own with him. He smiled and pulled some of the cloaks over them.

But she tilted her face up to be kissed and soon they no longer felt the cold in this room, or hear the noises from the halls or cared much about the distant explosions still rumbling through the tunnels. Time passed before they began to remove the other's clothes, almost timidly working through their layers until her lips touched his skin. His impressive knowledge of a woman's body deserted him and each touch was a new discovery, a permission asked and a permission granted. Their recent rough lovemaking aboard the *Dutchman* felt like an exercise in physical release compared to this tender embrace. They remained entwined and silent long after the last blissful shudder had calmed.

He raised his head to kiss her softly. "Hell isn't so bad, is it?"

"Not when you're there."

"Friends?" he said. It was not an idle question this time. She smiled. "Friends."

ELEVEN

Hours later Seth made his way through a tangle of sleeping or at least resting prisoners to find Caelyn among them. He had to resort to pinching the Delphian's ear before reaching him in that fathomless depth that his people called sleep. The Bellac who had curled up next to Caelyn mumbled in protest when he sat up, blinking tiredly.

"Is it time to go?" he said, disoriented.

Seth gestured for him to follow. They left the prisoners and went to the storage room where Nova still slept.

Caelyn went to her at once. "What's wrong with her?" He knelt beside their makeshift pallet and put his hand on her forehead. She was breathing in shallow gasps and her pale lips were as blue-tinted as his own.

"She needs medicine. It's on the *Dutchman*. We didn't exactly intend to spend the night here and I suppose we both forgot. She'll suffocate without it."

"She needs oxygen?"

"Yes."

Caelyn raised an eyebrow. "You do realize that an energetic act of copulation will burn a great deal of oxygen, right?"

Seth had the grace to blush. But there was no point in explaining to the Delphian that, to Nova, responding to fear and anger with a bout of sex was as curative as laughter after escaping a horde of Rhuwacs. "Can you help her?"

"I can try to slow her down a little. Keeping her cold will help." He pulled away all but one blanket, then turned to study Seth for a moment. "Maybe it's time to give yourselves up to whoever is chasing you. The Air Command force here will have medics. And oxygen. Whatever you did isn't worth risking her life."

"We can't do that. We have to get to Naiya. And you know that the Union will not just let us go there on our own."

"Then leave her here!"

"We can't do that, either. She's carrying your catalyst."

Caelyn stared at him, shocked. "What?"

"The tank you were shipping on the *Dyona* broke and the Naiyad transferred the catalyst to her before it died. It's what's killing her now. It wasn't this bad before. We have to get back to my ship."

"Go. Get ready." Caelyn turned to Nova and placed a hand on her chest, over her heart, the other on her forehead. His thumb rested on the neural interface at her temple. He closed his eyes. "She's Human. I have no idea if this is going to work, so you better hurry."

Seth went to rouse some of the women and then bundled up to leave the relative safety of the cargo area. The skimmer he investigated was serviceable and he programmed a low but tolerable temperature before returning to the building carved into the cliff. By the time he got there, Nova was awake and fairly coherent and had traded her clothes for some of the prison garb. Seth, too, removed his weather gear and shared it with the prisoners in exchange for a battered one-piece and a tattered cloak long enough to hide his guns.

Finally he pulled the *Dutchman*'s com unit from his upper arm and sat down to reprogram it. Nova crawled into his lap as he did so and buried her face in the curve of his neck.

"There's my fearsome warrior," he said lightly but threw a worried glance at Caelyn. She was cold and limp and each breath seemed a longer draw than the last.

"I'm going to transfer the ship's command codes to you, Caelyn," Seth said, holding his arms awkwardly around Nova to work with the device. "No one will suspect trickery from a Delphian. If we get caught tell them we're both ill with something nasty." He pushed his sleeve up to let a scanner on his data sleeve record the surface of Caelyn's hand. "Can you do this, Delphi?"

"Just hold up your end, Centauri."

Seth lifted Nova into his arms and they made their way to the loading dock door. Some of the captives came to see them off, gasping when a blast of wintry air pushed into the space. Caelyn invoked several of his many gods, unused to such temperatures even during the coldest of Delphian seasons. Nova made no sound when they walked down a short ramp to the waiting skimmer. The women closed the bay door behind them and they were left in the frozen landscape, hearing only the ceaseless wind howling through the canyons. There were no sounds of battle out here, nor did they see airships above.

"I hope they haven't all gone already," Caelyn said. He waited for Seth to climb into the car's passenger seat and then deposited Nova into his lap.

Seth linked his neural interface to the skimmer while the Delphian took the helm. "Head north along the bottom of the cliff," he instructed, reading the vehicle's sensors. "There are about forty life forms up at Ge'en. Lots of hardware. Some of the ships are Union issue. Clean-up crew, probably."

Caelyn hovered the skimmer off the ground and they were soon racing northwards. He followed Seth's direction to climb the vehicle up along a ridge and toward the canyon sheltering the decrepit mining town. Seth groaned when he saw several armed guards near the *Dutchman*. One of them raised a hand along with her gun, the instruction clear.

Caelyn powered the vehicle down and raised the canopy. Nova grumbled unintelligibly when the gust of bitter air hit them. He wasted no time in climbing out of the skimmer, like most Delphians paying no heed to a gun in a Union soldier's hands. He walked to Seth's side of the car and took Nova from his arms. "Surely you are not going to stand in my way, young woman," he said to the soldier. "This Human is in need of immediate medical attention."

The Centauri did not move. "You'll have to identify yourself," she said, her voice muffled by the mask protecting her face. Another guard stopped Seth when he climbed out of the car.

Caelyn's expression was as cold as the wind biting their skin. "If you think that after weeks in this pit I have anything even remotely resembling whatever identification you feel is acceptable then perhaps you require additional training. I am FennTar Mo'ghar Chiet Phan Caelyn on a scientific expedition and I, along with my technicians, was abducted several weeks ago. My ship here was taken as well. Now if you will stand aside to let me reclaim my property and get these people to safety, you will have saved some lives today. However, I cannot guarantee that whatever is afflicting them isn't contagious."

She looked uncertainly at the disheveled woman hanging limply in Caelyn's arms. "Where are you taking them?"

"At this point I am hoping the medical department aboard whatever carrier has brought you here is better equipped than my ship. Beyond that is really none of your concern. If you are looking for something to do, you will find sixteen more captives waiting for help at the loading docks south of here. Up until now it would appear that none of your company has even managed to locate that exit. No wonder so many of these despicable rebels elude capture."

Seth groaned and slumped against the skimmer, surely close to fainting.

Caelyn looked worried. "Will you have these people freeze to death while you decide on protocol? You can contact our Clan Council on Delphi to establish my identity. They will be interested as to why I am being waylaid once again."

She scowled at him, clearly undecided. Detaining an already badly mistreated Delphian could easily damage the Union's careful maneuverings to improve their fragile alliance with that planet. Hostility on her part would undoubtedly be reported, as Caelyn's veiled threat had made clear.

At last she waved him away. "Proceed directly to the base ship in orbit. I'll advise them of your arrival and make sure you are received by a medical team as a possible hazmat situation. Do not deviate from a direct course there."

"Thank you, officer," Caelyn said in a dignified tone. He walked the few steps to the *Dutchman* and pressed his hand to its key plate as if he did so daily. "And please be sure to evacuate those captives immediately. Some of them also require medical attention."

Seth lurched into the cargo bay and waited impatiently for Caelyn and Nova before raising the ramp. "Laid that on kind of thick, didn't you?" he said as the decon scan inspected them for things not wanted aboard the ship. He then ushered Caelyn into the cabin where the Delphian placed Nova carefully onto the lounger.

Caelyn grinned. "That was exhilarating. I may have a future as a spy."

Seth rummaged through a box until he found Nova's supply of medicine vials. He pushed her ragged sleeve past her elbow and, when his numb hands refused to cooperate, opened one of the packages with his teeth. "Spy?"

"Centauri, if you're a rebel I have to tell you that you're currently fighting on the wrong side. Is she a double agent, too?"

Seth shook his head. "Regular army." He held the ampoule to Nova's arm, hesitating until Caelyn took it out of his hand and nudged him out of the way. "When did you figure it out?" Seth said.

The Delphian quickly and efficiently administered the drug while Seth pulled blankets around her. "When you shot that rebel. Your loathing for them and their kind shines like a beacon. I don't even need to touch your mind to feel that." He looked down at Nova. "And my head isn't clouded by all those high emotions Humans suffer from."

"Didn't think you Delphians were quite so empathic." Seth breathed on Nova's hands, feeling no response to any of their attentions.

"We're not! In fact, most of us are as dense as ordium in that area unless we can link up directly. We just pretend we don't care when really we just don't even understand what drives you people. But I had a remarkable mentor on Delphi before I turned to navigation."

Seth grinned. "I won't tell anyone." He stood up to fetch a bottle of oxygen.

"So why doesn't she know about you?" Caelyn asked when Seth crouched beside the lounger cubby to adjust a respirator over Nova's face.

"She probably suspects," he said. "She's in enough danger without my baggage. I'm Prime Staff. Baroch's."

Caelyn gasped. "Gods! I heard about those! I thought it was just a rumor. And you're working for the Delphian Factor? Baroch himself? How did that come about? And how, by Mel'bry's beard, does Prime Staff get interested in our Naiya-saving mission?"

Seth shrugged. "Let's get out of here. And the less you know the better."

"Seth," Nova whispered.

He took her hands in his to stop her from pulling the oxygen mask away. "I'm here, Red."

She opened her eyes, barely able to keep awake. "I'd like to know, too."

* * *

When Nova awoke the cabin was quiet. Something blipped to itself in the cockpit and the soft whirr of the life support systems indicated that they were in-flight. She stretched and rolled over, pleased to feel that strength had returned to her limbs, to look at Seth lying beside her.

He slept on his side and she observed him for a long while, easily done without the violet eyes to distract her with their observant, ever-sardonic intensity. It was a gentle face, she decided, so slightly not-Human, and so slightly illusory for all that she didn't know about him but thought she did. She leaned close to him and kissed his lips.

He smiled after a moment and draped his arm loosely over her waist without opening his eyes. Reluctantly, Nova rose from the lounger, not without a few winces and groans, and padded into the coffin-sized hygiene compartment near the cargo area.

He was up when she emerged again and she took a few pieces of clothing from him. "How do you feel?" he asked when she had slipped into tights and a wonderfully soft and baggy shirt.

"New," she said. "Clean. Awake. Alive. How long was I out for?"

"Quite a while. But it's a long trip, so you didn't miss much except for Caelyn's weird chanting sessions."

Nova went into the galley in desperate need of very hot tea. "Where is he?"

"Resting. He found a keyhole before we even got to Aram gate and we were able to jump all the way past Magra. It knocked him out but we've saved two days' travel time."

"I slept through that? What happened on Aram?"

He shrugged and took a cup from her. "We just left. The Eagles had gone already and they didn't have anything left that can catch the *Dutchman*. They wouldn't bother to send the base ship after us. Probably figured we were rebels making an escape."

She inhaled the soothing fragrance of the tea. "And? Are we?"

"Nova..."

She held up a hand. "Yes, Prime Staff, I get that. Way too

much secret stuff for this lieutenant. But you didn't have to let me believe you're a rebel. Although now I know how you got out of that scrape on Targon so easily. And how you got the upgrades for the *Dutchman*. Does Carras know who you are?"

Seth nodded. "Sort of. He's probably been told enough to look the other way. I doubt he trusts me a whole lot."

"Should he?"

"Don't make me lie anymore."

"Then don't! Can you not trust me?"

"I have my orders, too, Lieutenant."

"And what are those?" she said, refusing to budge.

He put his cup down and turned to walk away before remembering that there was little chance of escape on the small ship. She propped her elbows on the galley counter to watch him pace about. He fiddled with the air system, then turned on some music before returning to sit at the galley counter.

"I was working on Colonel Drackon," he said finally. "There's been suspicion about him for a while and the Factors asked me to investigate. Mostly gun running, embezzlement, that sort of thing. I didn't know why they'd be interested in this but you don't question the Factors."

"And then you realized that he was working with rebels, not just moving the stuff on the side. The Factors must have suspected that or they wouldn't have sent you on this."

"Yes. I was already working my way up to Pe Khoja and pretty much embedded on Magra. He confirmed that Drackon was using rebels for black ops against Union interests. Mostly for profit. Then you came along and I had to consider that Carras might be in on this, too, as much as I didn't want to. That would compromise the entire Targon base."

She nodded. "And then Drackon drops Rellius' name and suddenly it's clear why they'd use Prime Staff for this case. They're not just after Drackon. They're after one of their own." She cocked her head. "And still you are working to keep Naiya out of Commonwealth hands."

"Yeah." He lifted a hand to cup her chin. "I'm a rebel."

She put a finger to his lips when he leaned over the counter to kiss her. "Is this why you left? Left me? Back then?"

He sighed and sat back down. "Nova, please..."

"I won't ask you about your work. But I think you owe me the truth where it concerns me. I am involved."

"Yes, it's why I left. I was already working for Intelligence, but not the Factors. There were rebels at the academy. Sabotage. Espionage. Nothing terribly interesting but when they made me the offer to join Prime Staff I took it. They were looking for unknowns. People that would stay unknown." He chewed on his lip. "You were the price of that."

"And you paid it."

"I did. I am not like you, Nova. I knew I'd never make it in your army. Was I going to work as a transport pilot somewhere? That didn't sound all that exciting. I was thinking about deep space exploration; they're always looking for a pilot crazy enough to head into the Badlands. But then I got this chance and I took it."

She came out of the galley space to stand close to him, between his knees, and wrapped her arms around his neck. "That I can understand. One more question and then I'll shut up."

"Hmm?" he said, his eyes on her lips and his hands on her bottom.

"Vincent and Acie?"

"Rebels both. But not Shri-Lan. Do not turn them in. They are more valuable to me outside than locked up somewhere."

She raised an eyebrow. "Oh? Giving orders now? Last I heard, Prime Staff is about as far removed from the military as you can get."

He pulled her closer. "Not feeling very far removed at this moment."

She burst into laughter when they heard the door to the crew cabin slide open. Seth muttered unhappily.

"Recovered?" Caelyn asked when he entered the cabin. "It's good to see you on your feet." He glanced at Seth's hands. "Although I see you have some help with that."

She stepped away from Seth. "So where are we now, anyway?"

"Still two days before we're in com range to the rebel base or whatever they have waiting for us at the keyhole to Naiya," Seth said. "We'll have to find a way to stall our approach till Caelyn can work out the math."

"Is the feeder interface going to work for you?" she asked Caelyn. She busied herself in the galley. "Anyone else want some food? I'm starving."

"If you're offering," Seth said.

"That interface is a joy to work with. I will be able to span that breach," Caelyn said. "But it won't be fast, so the sooner we can lock on the better. Oh, we also have to try your suit. I made some adjustments." He left them to go into the cargo hold. When he returned he was carrying her pressure suit. She let him help her pull it on while Seth took over her chores in the galley.

"What did you do?" Nova held her arm up. Caelyn had installed some sort of valve around the upper arm of her suit.

"I am assuming that you will have to offer up your blood, or the catalyst within it, once we're on Naiya. This will allow us to pull your sleeve off without leaking oxygen into the atmosphere. Or letting Naiya's elements into your suit."

"Except for my arm. Is that safe?"

"It's not ideal, but it isn't overly toxic. Hopefully, we won't be there long enough for you to absorb things through your skin. You should be all right."

"*Should?* How about we just stick a tube through the suit into my arm. Have you thought of that?"

"Yes, but given that there is no technology to speak of on Naiya, doing that won't remove the entire catalyst, only whatever is in the blood you spill. It was designed to be delivered by a Myrid. We have to rely on the Naiyads to know what they're doing."

"You have a lot of faith in a bunch of squid." She watched while he made adjustments to the valve. "That's tight!"

"It'll prevent you from bleeding out."

"What?"

Seth laughed. "And I thought Delphians have no sense of humor." He went into the cockpit and activated the communications console.

Nova peered at Caelyn. He avoided her eyes. "Make it tighter," she said before turning to see what Seth was doing. "Who are you messaging?"

"I'm not. You are. Time to give Daddy a call."

TWELVE

There was something eerie about the tense silence that had descended over the *Dutchman*, now just a few hours away from its destination. Nova had completed a check of its armaments and defense systems and now had little to do but fret. Most pilots operated their ships via a neural interface, leaving few tasks to manual controls and the likelihood of the errors that produced. The processors' unfailing accuracy ensured immediate results, barely delayed by safety algorithms, but watching Seth and Caelyn recline motionless on their benches was a little unnerving.

Data and charts shifted in three-dimensional displays above them, echoing the information fed to them by the system. The Delphian was preparing to detect the promised keyhole whose coordinates lay just ahead now. Seth monitored the farthest reaches of their scanners for the presence of others. The auto-pilot took care of their course. Only an occasional squawk emitted from the boards, no music played to distract them, and Nova tried to move as silently as possible.

"Found them," Seth finally said, startling Nova. Caelyn did not flinch, immersed so deeply in his mental exercise that little reached his consciousness. "The station, I mean."

She crouched by Seth's bench and put her hand on his leg to let him know she was there. His eyes remained closed. "Not far now. They have a lot of hardware. More than I thought. Carriers, floating platforms, transmitters, a few cruisers, fighters."

"Fighters? Out here? You mean Shrills?"

He nodded. "Dozens. They must be expecting trouble." His mental instruction to the *Dutchman* switched an overhead screen to an interpretation of the sensors' findings. "Should have real-vid soon."

"Could they have intercepted our packet?" They had spent much time over composing a message to her father, requesting a full Air Command assault on the rebel location. If they had deployed at once they would arrive in this sub-sector within hours. Enough of a distraction, hopefully, to let the *Dutchman* make a run for the contested keyhole before anyone guessed their intent.

"No. They know we're here. If they weren't happy about that we'd know by now."

"Any sign of our surprise visitors?"

Seth shifted the maps to include the jumpsite back into Trans-Targon, now hours behind them. No traffic showed on the grid. "Nothing yet. Let's hope your old man won't let you dangle in the breeze just to teach you a lesson. We can stall for just so long."

"He's not an ogre, you know. He'll have all of Targon mobilized after the news we gave him. I'm his favorite daughter by default." Nova watched Caelyn's immobile face for a few moments. "Is he finding anything yet?"

"Yes, he is," Caelyn said, awake after all. "But with the Centauri using every resource to just get there, I don't have much left for the central processor. So all I can do is look at the keyhole and admire it for its simple, mathematical perfection."

"Is he being sarcastic?" Nova whispered.

Seth smiled.

"Well," she sighed. "It's kind of boring watching you two lying around. Let me know if I can do anything."

"You can move your hand up by about that much," Seth said.

She slapped his thigh and straightened up.

Caelyn tilted his bench up and came to his feet. "I am going to meditate a while to prepare. And perhaps pray to what gods are still watching us out here that you people know what you're doing. I take comfort knowing that Celessa thinks the catalyst transfer will work, but how you'll get us past the rebels is a mystery to me. Hopefully she'll—" He halted abruptly when he saw Nova's face. His eyes traveled to Seth. "Why are you looking at me like that? Something isn't right with what I said."

"Caelyn," Nova began and looked to Seth for help.

"What's happened?" Caelyn said. "Is she all right?"

Nova winced. "No, she isn't. I'm sorry, Caelyn. The lab on Tyra was attacked. Two cruisers came not long after we got there. We tried to head them off but they destroyed the building."

Caelyn had gone very pale and there was no expression on his face she could interpret. "The lab is gone? All of them?"

"Yes. There was nothing left. We took out the two attack ships. Caelyn, I'm so sorry! We did tell her you were alive and that we'd try to find you. She was worried about that." Nova faltered. What could she possibly say to him that would make any of this better?

"Drackon," he said tonelessly.

"Probably."

He took a deep breath and exhaled slowly. "And the Naiyad is gone, too, then. There was only one left. So you have the last of the catalyst."

She nodded.

He stared into space for a moment and then retreated into the crew cabin, closing the door softly behind him.

"Caelyn," Nova called after him.

"Leave him be," Seth said.

She sighed. "He must feel terrible. *I* feel terrible."

"Leave him. They have their ways of dealing with things like this."

She absolutely did not want to leave Caelyn to grieve alone, but what did she know about Delphians? Seth, on the other hand, had spent his life studying the species that shared their space. If any outsider had a notion about the secretive ways of these people, it would be him. "I'll get our equipment ready," she said. "I don't suppose we'll need weapons on Naiya. Did you fill the air tanks?"

She busied herself, checking things they'd already checked, her thoughts on Caelyn. It always seemed to be the civilians that took the brunt when their worlds clashed. While armies fought in the sky, the people on the ground paid the price. Killed, dispossessed, tortured, enslaved. She had seen it on Bellac, on Nebdan, and any other place to which she had been assigned. How often had she met people, come to like them, only to have them disappear from her life again? They had rescued Caelyn only to put him into great danger again. Acie and Vincent risked their lives every time they worked with Seth. Would they still be on Magra if she returned there? Nova set aside the air hoses she was sorting, went into the cockpit, and leaned down to kiss Seth.

He opened his eyes. "I deserved that, I'm sure."

She smiled. "And more."

"Incoming message," he said suddenly.

Indeed, a low and persistent sound emitted from the com console, demanding their attention. Nova stepped closer to it and opened a channel. "*Dutchman,*" she said, in an unknown part of space and in conversation with people who required no formal identification.

"About time," she was greeted.

"Having tea still. What do you want?"

"A bit more speed out of you. Why are you crawling along out there? Where's Kada?"

"Busy."

"Tell him to get his crossdrives motivated. Drackon is about ready for an embolism if we don't get this gate open."

"Will be about an hour or two, standard time," she said. "Maybe three. This barge wasn't built for speed, you know." She winked at Seth, who snarled at this insult.

"We'll send a welcome party, *Dutchman*. It'll help you hurry."

She frowned. "We don't need a tow."

"Drackon insists. It's the polite thing to do. Base out."

Nova closed the channel before cursing. "Why are they sending an escort? There just isn't any way we can stall if they're shepherding us."

"Drackon is still there?" Seth said. A slow grin tugged on his lips. "Isn't that interesting."

"They'll make us dock at the station. I'm not at all interested in that. So much for running for that keyhole while they're not looking." Nova perched on the co-pilot bench and studied his thoughtful expression. "You're thinking something, Kada. Possibly something terribly irresponsible. Am I right?"

"Yes. Go dress like a rebel."

* * *

"That thing is massive!" Nova marveled when they arrived just hours later. "For a rebel outpost, anyway."

Displayed on the *Dutchman*'s main screen, the mismatched assembly of vehicles, joined by platforms and connective tunnels, formed a base station in what appeared to be absolutely nowhere. Three massive carriers faced inward to allow easy access for the Shri-Lan fighter planes, the agile and deadly Shrills. Several cruisers were docked to the bays, no doubt transporting supplies and personnel. The nearest, even marginally habitable planet was not even accessible in real-space from here. Two of the small, disk-shaped survey vessels used for charting expeditions hovered near the locks.

"This must cost a fortune to maintain all the way out here. We probably paid for every piece." Nova pointed at the screen. "Look, that array is military issue."

"What is that for?" Caelyn said. He had rejoined them this past hour, looking relaxed and composed. Nova, often at odds with her own temperament, marveled at this composure. Famously a Delphian trait, this ability to veil their emotions resulted in the cool detachment that others often found plainly irritating. Today she realized the value of it.

"Shield generators," she replied. "This platform's awfully close to the keyhole. But that array won't just shield it from the breach radiation. It'll also defend the place against EM weaponry."

Seth nodded. "Whoever's coming will have to skip the light show."

Caelyn studied the map suspended above them. Still nothing moved near the terminus to Trans-Targon, leaving them alone out here with the rebels. "*If* they're coming," he said. "How much longer can we stall?"

"You worry too much," Seth said. "If Air Command doesn't get here, we'll need to create some other distraction. If needed, you can work with their spanners for a while. No one will harm you. We just need to find a way to get Nova through the breach."

She looked at him sideways. "Is that all? This whole station was put here to stop the catalyst from getting through."

The Shrills that had escorted them to the station veered away, leaving them a little more at ease when the weapons lock indicator on the console dimmed again. Even the heavily-shielded *Dutchman* would not long withstand a sustained attack by a swarm of these ships.

"*Dutchman*, when you're done prancing around out there, pog into Seven."

"Just taking a tour," Seth said. "You have a lovely home."

The reply was an oath that made even Nova wince.

Caelyn shook his head, resigned to the company he was forced to keep. "If I ever see my beautiful planet again I will have to enter a year-long retreat just to get all of you out of my system." He poked a finger at the keyhole marker on their charts. "I don't suppose you've given any thought of how we might actually get back from Naiya without some very angry rebels shooting at us?"

"How did I know you'd find the flaw in my plan?" Seth said. He eased the *Dutchman* into the assigned docking port and they soon felt the usual, peculiar disorientation as the ship's gravitational field tried to match that of the station.

A few armed rebels, mostly Centauri and Feydan, watched suspiciously when Nova and Seth emerged with their prisoner. Nova stepped onto the dock first, an unpleasant sneer on her face. She had wrapped her easily-recognized hair in a scarf and then topped it with an interesting cap found among Seth's things. Like him, she wore leather trousers, heavy boots, a plain, sleeveless black shirt showing well-toned arms and a fake tattoo that Seth had patched on just for fun. Fearing that Drackon would recognize her, she had darkened her face to a shade common on Feyd and applied more of the temporary tattoos to her cheeks and neck.

Caelyn was back in his prison rags, his hands tied and his face expressionless. Nova had insisted on disheveling his hair which now frayed from his normally neat braid to hang over his face and shoulders.

"Delivery for Drackon," Seth said.

They seemed to have passed some sort of inspection when a Centauri rebel holstered his gun and jerked his chin toward the exit of the docking bay. "About time you showed up. We're getting tired of listening to the old man asking for you every hour."

Nova looked past the rows of pressure doors to see the colonel, incongruous in civilian garb, walk toward them, looking irritable even at this distance. Armed men walked by his side. Nova tried to see beyond their casual dress to detect the bearing of trained soldiers. How many of these rebels were not actually rebels?

She lowered the rim of her cap a little more and kept her face down as she nudged Caelyn forward with her gun. Seth walked in front of her, stopping again when an umbilical leading to one of the docked ships beside the *Dutchman* activated. Three men and a woman, all of them Human, emerged, looking like they just returned from some unimaginably long journey. Nova peered into the walkway to see the markings of the survey ship. These, then, were some of the cartographers pressed into service by Drackon.

The colonel, too, stopped to watch the team leave the docking area before approaching Seth. Nova stepped back and leaned against a bulkhead, looking bored as she watched someone unload a cruiser behind them. Some of the female rebels, mostly Centauri, looked truly frightening to her.

Drackon did not even glance in Nova's direction but looked up at Caelyn with proprietary interest. "That the spanner?"

Caelyn glowered at him, making no effort to disguise his loathing. His tone, however, was civil. "I must formally protest. Delphi will be outraged over this. You cannot expect me to cooperate in any way."

Drackon was unimpressed. "You'll see things my way sooner or later, protest all you want."

One of his men grasped the thick collar that bound Caelyn's hands. "You can leave the Delphi with us and be on your way back home," he said to Seth.

Seth's eyebrows twitched into a fleeting frown. "Not till we get paid," he said. "A thousand flash mods for Pe Khoja is what we're picking up."

"They're still on my ship, ready to be offloaded," Drackon said. "And there'll be no more for him. Make sure he knows it." He gestured to his guards. "Put the Delphi to work with the other spanners. I'll be along in a while. He's going to join the chartjumpers out near the keyhole. I want the span mapped and the charts in my hands within the next two hours. If he decides not to cooperate find a way to convince him. Delphis bleed like everybody else."

Caelyn looked back over his shoulder as he was led away, wordlessly pleading for help until one of his guards jammed a gun in his ribs him to move him along.

Seth and Nova followed when the colonel started to walk away, too. "You'll never get him to work for you," Seth said, keeping his voice low. "Any Delphian would rather jump out of an airlock than do something they don't see the need to. And they don't see the need for most rebel business. Or Union, for that matter. Your thugs have no idea how to handle one of them. I do. We'll come along to give them a hand."

"Not necessary," Drackon said. "I've got my own experts. The Delphi will cooperate. We're done here. Pick up the flash mods and leave."

At his gesture, two of his men barred the way, preventing Seth and Nova from following the colonel any farther than the gate to the docks.

Seth cursed under his breath when he and Nova returned to the *Dutchman*. Once back aboard, they engaged the ship's scanning systems to find where Caelyn might have been taken. Superstructure, compartments, the biosignatures of the people aboard, everything was scrutinized and analyzed in detail.

"Nothing," Nova said after a while, wishing they had equipped Caelyn with a tracker. "Can't tell anyone from anything. Isn't there anything different about a Delphian we can scan for?"

"Not really. Their body temperature is about two degrees cooler but I'm not getting any of that." He reached up to switch an overhead screen to create a physical map of the awkward conglomeration of ships and spare parts that made up this base. "What a mess," he sighed. "Not even a video system we can tap into."

She nodded. "Empty rooms, halls going nowhere, lifts that don't work, access tubes going every which way. That there looks like residentials. It's a wonder the whole thing hasn't collapsed by now. Look at this, though. If we're assuming the antenna arrays are forward of the shield generator, the cartography lab should be over on that side somewhere. They'll be running the sensors non-stop."

He nodded. "I don't like the idea of Caelyn actually spanning that keyhole without you there. If they get to Naiya before we do I can't see how we'll get a chance to use the catalyst."

"We better get busy, then."

"Let's split up. Check out your theory about the lab. I'll see if I can find something to blow up."

"Let's hope we don't have to resort to that," she said. "It wouldn't take much crumple this whole station like a box of biscuits." She terminated the sensor sweeps. "I hope they're not beating him to get him to cooperate. He's probably never had to deal with that before. I feel awful for dragging him into this."

"Celessa and her people dragged him into this." Seth left the cockpit to rummage through a gear bin in the main cabin. "Delphians belong on Delphi, not mixed up with rebels and traitor Union officers."

"There were some sharp Delphian pilots on Bellac," she said. "Not on my squad but I heard about them. They're not all scientists and flute players."

"They used to be. Keep this open." He gave her a com set and watched her tuck the speaker into her ear. A faint ticking assured them that their link had not yet been detected by another device. "Be careful."

She nodded and turned to the door but he caught her arm. "Listen, we have no room for error now. If you find him, get back here at once. If things get ugly, take the *Dutchman* and go for the keyhole. Don't wait for me."

"What do you mean? I can't jump this thing by myself!"

"Caelyn can. You just point the *Dutchman* in the right direction, if it comes to that. Your mission is the catalyst."

She searched his face, worried. "And what's yours? What's going on in that renegade brain?"

"I can't leave here without at least trying to nail Drackon.

It has taken too long to get here. He will make a run back to Trans-Targon the moment he smells trouble. If he escapes now the entire operation was for nothing."

"So? With what we have he'll never work for the Union again. *And* you have grounds to investigate Rellius."

"Yes, but Drackon is as likely to join Tharron as he is to disappear forever. Someone with his clearance switching sides is unthinkable. I can't let him leave this platform."

She frowned and resisted enough to make a point when he wrapped his arms around her waist. "I don't suppose it'll make even a tiny bit of difference to ask you to be careful?"

"No." He kissed her.

She rolled her eyes and slipped out of his arms. "Let's go and see if we can get our Delphian back."

There was no one outside the *Dutchman*'s gate when they stepped out of the ship. Seth winked at her and strolled away, toward the distant locks leading to the adjoining ship. Nova looked after him for a moment before heading into the opposite direction.

She walked quickly and with purpose, trying to look like any of the rebels working on this outpost. She ducked a few individuals who, by their bearing, appeared to be in charge of things. How did these people ever stay organized without rank or uniform? The concourse led into the residential wings as shown on the *Dutchman*'s maps but there was no one here now. She tried a few doors and found them unlocked with little of interest behind them.

Eventually she found an open lift leading to what she assumed to be the launch bay. A few pilots arrived on this level and she nearly ran into them when they stepped out of the elevator, distracted by their conversation.

"Whoa, almost ran you down, Princess."

She looked at him suspiciously, but the Human returned her glare with a friendly smile. "We're supposed to meet Kaycia on Two, in case you haven't heard," he said, gesturing back the way she came. "Some exercise going on."

She looked down the hall. "I know," she said and lowered

her voice. "But I was hoping to catch up with my boyfriend before we head out. I just got here and don't really know the place. I kind of got turned around."

"Is he a pilot?"

"No, he's one of the chartjumpers working on Drackon's project. Would you know where they are?"

A Centauri beside them snorted in derision. "I don't know how those professors do it." He allowed his eyes a little playtime over Nova's shirt. "Lucky guy."

His companion laughed. "You're in the right area, but the wrong hall. Go to the end of this one, head left and up the metal stairs to the left again. The chart lab is up there."

She smiled and slipped around them to follow his directions. "Did you get that?" she murmured once she was out of earshot. "Found the place."

"Did," Seth replied into her earpiece. "Sounds like you have a way with rebels."

Nova tapped the nearly undetectable microphone at her collar, knowing it would send an annoying scraping sound into his ear. She wandered down the hallway until she found the staircase and made her way up. Hushed voices led her to an open double-door. She stepped into the room, her boyfriend story ready.

What she saw were five or six technicians sitting on the floor against a long console, staring up at her like a row of startled birds, their eyes and mouths agape when she entered. She looked around, puzzled. No one was at the workstations or working with the displayed charts on the walls and holo tables. "Um, what's going on here?"

"We're not doing any more work on this!" one of the people on the floor said. She tried very hard to look defiant and courageous. "So don't you wave your gun at us!"

Nova came closer, her weapon firmly holstered at her side. "Wasn't going to. What are you doing on the floor?" She halted when two of the technicians drew together in fear. "Did they bring a Delphian here? Would have been just a short while ago."

"What do you want with him? You're too late."

"Too late?"

A Centauri pointed a shaking finger past Nova. When she turned she saw streaks of blood on the otherwise spotless floor. A long smudge of blood also ran along the wall to the door. "Oh, no," she gasped. "What did they do to him?"

"He refused to work with us. They tried to make him, of course. They beat him although that didn't seem to make much difference to him. Then they took him away. There is a detention area below here, near the hangars." The cartographer looked nervously at her coworkers. "We won't continue this work. Even if they beat all of us."

Nova started to turn away but then hesitated. "You people aren't even rebels, are you?"

"Certainly not! We were hired for a charting expedition. Nothing said about rebels or working insane hours or not being allowed to leave until the job's done. No response to our request for a Level Three to get the job done instead of having to crawl our way through. And now this!" She pointed at the blood spatters.

"Help is on the way," Nova promised.

"Nova..." came Seth's warning over her earpiece.

"These are civilians," she hissed. The technicians looked at her quizzically.

"What is your mission, Nova?" he said.

She ground her teeth and ignored him. "Do you people have access to the com from here?" She walked to the console. "Get up already!"

They came to their feet, unsure of what to do next. The Caspian went to the far end of the room. "We communicate with the survey vessels from here," he said.

"Good," Nova strode to the unit and examined its interface. "We have requested help from Air Command to rout this place. At some point, things will get noisy. When that happens, I want you to use this relay to keep sending warnings that there are civilians on this station. It'll make them more careful about where they shoot."

"So you think," Seth grumbled into her ear.

Her hands sped over the interface to isolate a com channel, suspecting that Seth was also remembering the attack on Aram at this moment. "Can you do this?"

"Yes, we'll keep sending."

"Not too soon."

"Yes. Who are you?"

She waved the question away. "Just do as I said. And stay here, together."

She left them to rush back down the stairs, back down the hall and back to where she had met the pilots by the lift. Impatiently, she waited for a platform and leaped onto it as soon as it arrived. "How are you making out," she whispered to Seth.

"Making my way around to your side of the platform. Gravity is a joke over here. No sign of Drackon or his men and no one's seen them. Of course I can't pretend I'm dating him. I hear he's happily married."

Nova grinned and jumped from the lift before it had even touched down. The lower level opened onto the launching pads for the Shrills. There was an archway beside the lift and she peered into the hallway beyond. She had to stifle her laughter when she saw that someone had taken a laser and burned a crude sketch of prison bars on the wall, behind which sat a stick figure with the word 'Tharron' above it. "I think I've found the detention area." She drew her gun and made her way down the hallway.

When she turned a corner she was only steps away from a guard loitering in a small antechamber facing two cells, busily carving some words into a plastic table top. He looked up when she entered. Behind him Caelyn sprawled on a metal bench inside one of the rooms. She lowered her weapon.

"Came to relieve you," she said, searching her mind for the name she had heard earlier. "Kaycia wants your group topside."

"She does?"

"Better hurry. You know how she can get."

He jerked his thumb toward the Delphian. "He's been quiet. Might be passed out." He handed her a short truncheon. "Give him a few wallops now and again to see if he's in the mood to get along with us. He won't fight back."

Caelyn stirred when he heard their voices and sat up on his bench with effort. His face was puffed and bleeding, partially obscured by his blood-soaked hair. He grunted in pain as he came to his feet.

Nova looked back at the guard, furious. "This is the best you people can do? Beat up unarmed civilians?" She raised her weapon. "You know, you're not going to live out this day anyway."

"Huh?" the rebel said before Nova's gun relieved him of duty.

She looked down at the fallen body for a moment before moving to Caelyn's cell. "Turn away," she snapped. The lock sprang open under the assault of her weapon. "Can you walk? Seth, I have him."

"Good, head back to the *Dutchman*."

She looked around and found a jug of liquid. She sniffed it and decided it was tea. Tearing a strip of cloth from Caelyn's shirt, she soaked it and wiped the worst of the blood from his face. "Are you all right?"

"I'm sure it looks worse than it is." He touched his swollen lip and winced. "Where is Sethran?"

"I have no idea. Let's get you back to the ship. He'll meet us there. I hope." She put her gun on the table and started to tidy up his hair. "Put my cap on to hide that eye. It's turning purple. Let's grab this guy's coat. You're all bloody."

"Gods!"

She turned into the direction of his startled gaze. Three men had rounded the corner into the detention room, Colonel Drackon among them. They came to a sudden stop when they saw the body on the floor, the Delphian out of his cell, and Nova by his side.

Before any of them had recovered from this surprise, Caelyn snapped up Nova's gun. "You!" He held her gun uneasily in both hands, pointed at Drackon's head. "You killed my sister!"

"What's going on," Nova heard Seth's anxious voice over the speaker in her ear.

Drackon backed away. His own men had raised their guns, looking far less nervous, both Caelyn and Nova in their sights. Nova, too, had drawn a second weapon, also aimed at the colonel although her eyes were on his men. "Put that gun down, Delphi," Drackon said. "I killed no one's sister."

"She was on Tyra when you sent your ships to destroy the lab," Caelyn said, any trace of his gentle voice erased. "She's dead by your orders."

"I'm almost there," Seth said, breathless. "Caelyn sounds like he snapped."

"Caelyn," Nova said, hoping to give Seth more time. "Give me that gun. You don't want to do this."

"Yes, I do, Nova."

Drackon's brows drew together. "Nova?" he said. "You're Nova Whiteside. The girl with the catalyst. Out here?"

Just then a sharp beam of light cut into the space from the corridor. The guard closest to Nova dropped to the ground. The other spun to shoot at Seth still out in the hall and she heard him yell in pain. His return fire took the rebel down. She grabbed her gun from Caelyn and shoved him back into his cell, barely ducking a bullet from Drackon's pistol before turning back to fire at the colonel. His body convulsed in a painful spasm as he crashed to the ground.

"Seth!" She rushed into the corridor to find him leaning up against the wall. A long scorch mark ran along the side of his leg.

"Just a little fried," he said through gritted teeth. "Is Caelyn still with us?"

"Yes. Just beat up. He'll be fine."

Seth limped after her into the detention area. "Is he dead?" he asked when Nova bent over the colonel.

"No." She looked up at the wall where Drackon's bullet

had buried itself. "What idiot uses a projectile weapon on a barge like this? I'd be surprised if they had any interior shielding at all."

Seth put his hand on Caelyn's shoulder as if to shake him out of his daze. "What happened?"

The Delphian blinked as if he had trouble understanding the question. "I... I'm sorry. I could not bear to look upon that man. I... I don't know what came over me."

"You had good reason," Seth said. "She really was your sister? That wasn't just a title?"

Caelyn nodded. "Yes, our Elder Sister really was my older sister. We often joked..." He sighed and fell silent.

Nova rose and reached around him, not surprised when he did not return her embrace. She pressed her cheek to his chest anyway. "I'm so sorry, Caelyn. We'll get you home. I promise."

He smiled sadly. "That just doesn't seem very likely right now."

An alarm sounded on the main concourse, ringing through the halls with strident urgency. "What the hell..." Nova rushed into the hallway. People hurried in several directions, shouting advice and questions at each other. Two of them collided, nearly taking down a third, reminding her more of panicked civilians than a trained rebel force.

"Get to your station," someone snapped at her. "Air Command just dropped in on us. They'll be here in a few hours. We're launching all fighters."

"Air Command!" she exclaimed. "That's terrible! Who's aboard?"

"They are silent. One carrier and three Eagles, but it's the *Zoya* out of Targon. One hundred Union fighters and her armaments are beyond what we can handle. If she gets past our Shrills we don't stand a chance here on this platform." He spun and jogged away.

Nova hurried back to Seth and Caelyn. "Carras is here. We need to get to the *Dutchman*."

Seth prodded Caelyn toward her. "I'll lock the colonel up

down here and get the rest of these heaps out of sight. He'll be out for a few more hours so this should keep him in place. You two get to the *Dutchman* and prepare to launch. Act like you're joining the battle. I'll only slow you down. Get Caelyn plugged in."

"We can help you get back," Nova said.

"Go! Caelyn will need time to get ready for the jump. I'll get there." He smiled crookedly. "Well, hopefully. If I'm not there by the time the defense launches, just go. I'll take my chances with the civilians."

"You just hope Carras won't smash this wreck into bits." Nova grabbed Caelyn's arm and dragged him into the passageway. She dodged people right and left as they hurried past the hangar and into the lift, praying to several gods that weren't especially native to her species that no one would stop them. The levels above were nearly deserted until she reached the small craft bays. Some of the other pilots were also getting ready to join the battle. At this point she was prepared to shoot the first rebel who dared to stand in her way.

No one did. Once aboard, she paused to appreciate the sweet sound of the *Dutchman*'s gate slamming shut before digging through the cold storage compartment for something to cool Caelyn's bruises. Holding the compress to his face, he tilted the co-pilot couch and engaged his neural interface to prepare for the jump they planned to make.

Like the pilots on both sides of the *Dutchman*, Nova started her pre-fight checks, silently fretting over Seth. She cursed under her breath when the minutes ran by like seconds and there was still no sign of Seth. The lights in the corridor had turned orange; soon someone would activate the airlock hatches and they'd be forced to launch without him. She scanned the halls with the ship's exterior cameras as if doing so every few minutes would hasten his arrival. "Where the hell is he?"

"Don't be swearing like that in front of the Delphian," came Seth's calm voice over her earpiece. She heard the ship's gate open behind her. "He's delicate."

THIRTEEN

"All right, are we ready for this?" Seth gripped the headrests of the pilot and co-pilot's chair and vaulted into his seat. "Caelyn? Are you feeling it?"

The Delphian, already secured for the flight, nodded. His half-closed eyes were focused on nothing and he did not react when Nova leaned over him to shift the gun controls to the right side of the cockpit. "I have the coordinates and the keyhole. Such a long reach..."

"Can you make it?" Nova asked. She threw Seth a worried glance as she turned over the cooling pad on Caelyn's cheek. The possibility that Caelyn might fail to span the breach in his current state of mind had not even occurred to her. Even the least talented of chartjumpers spanning the safest of jumpsites needed utter concentration to guide his machine during a subspace leap.

"Guess we'll find out," Seth said. He engaged his own interface and released the docking clamps. A mild push of the thrusters allowed the *Dutchman* to drop away from the station. Two rebel cruisers prowled nearby but nothing else moved out here.

"How far out are they?" Nova asked.

Seth directed the scanners toward the keyhole leading to Trans-Targon. Symbols appeared beside the markers for the approaching Air Command ships. "Making tracks! An hour, maybe two. I guess Daddy pushed a few buttons; Targon doesn't take that boat on many pleasure cruises."

"Told you he likes me."

"Mentioning Drackon probably helped," Seth said. He cringed away from her exaggerated scowl. "Not that you're not worth launching battleships for!"

"Dutchman!" someone snapped over the open com. "What are you doing out here? The launch has not yet been called."

Seth let the ship drift vaguely in the direction of the keyhole to Naiya. "Wanted a front row seat," he said.

There was a moment of silence after someone shut the com link down. Then he was back. "Take position above the antenna arrays. Don't engage until ordered."

"Aye, sir," Seth said, continuing to drift. It took a moment before someone noticed.

"Did you hear me? What are you doing?"

Seth turned the *Dutchman* away from the station and the indicator before them turned orange when he powered up the shields. "Come on, Caelyn," he said. "We need this to happen."

Caelyn sprawled motionless on his bench, his mind locked to the *Dutchman*'s navigation system as he probed the unimaginable distance between the microscopic breach in space and its terminus. He felt his way while the ship calculated, looking for the exit as he methodically spanned the reach to show the *Dutchman* the way out again. "I'm almost there," he said, somehow sounding very far away. "It's so very unstable."

"That cruiser's heading our way," Nova said. "I think they know we're up to something."

"Dutchman, disengage from that keyhole. What are you doing?"

"Drackon's orders," Seth said. When Caelyn nodded he started to feed the keyhole, creating the energy field needed to power them through the breach. "He wants the thing mapped, doesn't he?"

"Now? Are you mad? Return to the platform."

"We'll be back in time for the party, don't worry."

"You are not cutting out, coward," the rebel said, sounding furious.

Nova grinned. "He thinks we're running away? Into an uncharted breach?"

"Beats getting blown to bits by Carras' boys, I guess," Seth said. "Damn, he's ramping up his guns." Seth dropped his pretense and accelerated the *Dutchman* toward the keyhole. It streaked away from the surprised rebel, soon exceeding the ship's original velocity limits.

"He's after us!" Nova leaned over Caelyn to take manual control over the weapons system. Indeed, a barrage of laser fire streaked past them, glancing off their shields.

"Now! Go!" Caelyn barked and Seth veered to punch the *Dutchman* directly at the expanding breach.

Nova realized that she had never jumped even a charted site while not at least hanging on to something more solid than the tactical controls. The ship plunged into nothing and she lost all perception of light or sound or even the floor beneath her feet. The tremendous vertigo of the moment seemed to turn the inside of her head upside down and she was no longer sure if she was even standing upright.

When she could see again she was on the floor, crumpled beneath the com console with a new pain blooming between her shoulder blades. "Seth!"

"I'm on it," he said, shaking his head to clear the fog of this tremendous journey from his mind. He gained control of the careening *Dutchman* to slow the ship and get his bearings. "I think we made it."

Something slammed into their aft shields and Nova lurched forward despite the *Dutchman*'s rock-solid gravity matrix. "He came through with us," she said. "Bastard doesn't know when he's not wanted."

The *Dutchman* came about and she unleashed several of Seth's military-grade missiles upon the rebel ship. Either too slow or too surprised, their pursuer had no chance to return her fire before his ship broke up, scattering pieces of itself in a wide swath behind them. Nova hooted gleefully. "We make a team, don't we?"

Seth grinned. "We do." He switched their scanners to deal with a dust cloud floating through this sub-sector. "Look at that," he said.

A gently pulsing beacon on the three-dimensional map showed the way to Naiya, not far ahead now. "It's right here. I can see why Rellius is so excited about the place. Barely any real-space travel needed."

Nova bent over Caelyn. He breathed evenly, slowly, eyes closed. The blue brows were drawn together as if in pain or concentration. "Caelyn? Are you still with us?"

He nodded but did not open his eyes. "Did we make the jump all right?"

Seth studied the reports from the *Dutchman*'s system check. Any jump put as much strain on the processors and shields as on the navigator and this had not been a simple traverse. Even a slight miscalculation on Caelyn's part could have lethal results. "We're all right. That jump chewed up a big chunk of my thorium. We're a long way from home."

Caelyn sat up to watch the real-vid display of the orange planet suspended in the light of a distant binary system. "We'll need to decon before stepping out. There hasn't been much opportunity to study the planet so I want to make sure we're clean." He sighed. "Most of the latest samples were on Tyra, so they're lost now anyway."

Nova nodded, surprised by the sorrow she heard in his voice. Perhaps she was beginning to understand the Delphian. Or perhaps he no longer cared to hide his feelings from them.

"Erratic orbit," Seth reported. "Pressure is fine so the enviro suits will do. No oxygen, gravity's a bit heavy, hotter than Feyd on a summer day. Super."

Nova dropped onto her heels and gripped his chair when they began their descend but the transition was smooth and they were not jolted too badly. Caelyn's landing coordinates guided them to an island near the planet's equator.

Naiya's dun-colored surface began to distinguish itself from the amber fluid that filled the oceans. Channels and rivers, vast bays and inland seas fissured the continents. An occasional outcropping of rock or heavily eroded crater pockmarked the otherwise featureless ground.

Seth hovered the *Dutchman* into a landing. A plume of dust rose up and hung in the air like fog.

"Is that what I think it is?" Nova said.

"Water ash. Just lying around like so much dust. Let's get suited up."

They helped Caelyn climb out of his chair. Still disoriented and exhausted from the incredible mental strain that the jump had demanded, he moved like a man three times his age. They pulled their gear from the cargo hold and climbed into it, taking their time while the dust settled around the ship. It was a while before all three were securely sealed into their cocoons and breathing bottled air. The last step was to subject themselves and the cargo area to a decontamination pass before meeting Naiya's open environment.

One by one they exited the ship and looked around themselves in wonder. As they walked to the ocean's edge, the powder under their heavy boots gave way and they sank ankle-deep before finding solid purchase. No waves rose above the thick fluid stretching to the curved, yellow horizon. Shifting bands of orange and amber light played over the sky, coloring the water ash floating like lace on the surface of the sea. They felt no wind against their bodies in this melancholy world. It was desolate and dull, even by Nova's spaceship-bound standards, and yet she sensed a warm, comfortable peace here as though nothing ever intruded upon the silence. She was certain that it was possible to sit by the shore for hours and never feel boredom or loneliness.

In the distance, an oddly shaped structure rose above the dull sheen. Narrow towers reached for the overcast sky, their superstructure gnarled and uneven as though encrusted with Class Three fauna. Or Class Five residents.

"Do you hear that?" Nova said.

"Yes," Seth replied. "But how?"

A constant sound hung in the air like a distant song or a breeze though some otherworldly chime, audible despite the sealed protection of their helmets.

"You're *feeling* that sound," Caelyn said. "It's from below. The Naiyads make it. They know we're here." He gestured back at the *Dutchman*. "The landing of ships here is painful to them. The vibration interferes with their song."

Nova stared out over the sea, content to remain standing forever on this lifeless expanse of shoreline but unsure why she felt that way. "This place is beautiful," she murmured.

"Wait till you see below," Caelyn said. "Come."

They followed him into the sea, not without some trepidation as they stepped deeper into the fluid. The ground dropped rapidly but there was little change in buoyancy. Nova took an involuntary and very deep breath when her helmet at last also submerged. She felt an assuring hand press against her back and turned to peer at Seth. His face was barely visible behind his visor but his expression echoed the wonder she felt.

The three travelers walked sluggishly through the honey-colored fluid, aware of a thousand points of light around them, unable to discover the source of any of it. Soon they saw a multitude of Naiyads glide toward them with undulating movements of their long limbs. In places the crowd was so dense that they looked like a seething mass of tentacles. The teeming bodies parted as if to outline a path along the lighter sea floor which the travelers followed.

Nova wondered how they could ever have thought of the Naiyads as squid. Many of them hovered at eye level and their boneless limbs reached nearly to the ground. A luminescent substance pulsed along these limbs in shades of pink and blue. The large, bulbous eyes observed them with evident curiosity.

"Are you getting anything but that singing, Caelyn?" Nova asked.

"Not so far," the Delphian replied, his calm voice undistorted by their sound system.

"Look," Seth said. "The way they move. This must be a sort of communication for them."

Indeed, some of the Naiyads' moved their nimble appendages in distinct patterns too complex to be merely accidental, tapping and stroking the limbs of their companions. No current moved here, yet some of the creatures undulated in synchronicity to express something far beyond their visitors' comprehension.

Nova moved as if in a dream. The substance in which they were immersed pressed against her body like warm oil but she felt afloat and her feet scarcely touched the ground. The song in her mind increased in volume but did not cease its hypnotic one-note effect. She turned to gaze at the display of color and light all around her and wondered if she was, indeed, asleep.

A few of the Naiyads approached them directly now and Caelyn lifted his hands toward them. His gloves were of a thinner material than Seth and Nova's equipment, substantial enough to protect him from this fluid, light enough to allow him communicate. One of the creatures swam up into his hands and settled there.

"We are greeted," he said when his mind touched the Naiyad's. "They are curious. Not hostile. I'm not sure they're capable of hostility. They think you are very hard to the touch."

Nova bent awkwardly to look at several of the Naiyads squelching around her boots. One or two of them swam up and she moved her hands through their limbs. "Are they going to bite me again?"

"Yes."

She withdrew her hand. "Do they know why we're here?"

"Not really. They do understand that your blood is important to them. They don't know what lies outside this world, but we've made them realize that they are in danger unless we release the catalyst. The Naiyads are intelligent but there is little point of reference for what we try to tell them." He gestured by sweeping a hand through the fluid. "They live in sort of a dream. You can feel that, I'm sure. It's like music. They live in music."

"What makes that music?" Seth asked.

"They do. A vocal apparatus in their heads. The songs are like thoughts or words that move through the fluid. They don't have much to say. They float, they eat, they sing, they mate."

Seth made a startled sound and staggered backward.

Nova turned to see that one of the cephalopods had attached itself to his helmet and another seemed about to do the same. "What are you doing?"

"What am I doing? What are *they* doing!" More of the creatures settled over his visor to obscure his vision completely. "They better not be mating on me. Stop laughing, Red."

Caelyn reached out and brushed the Naiyads from Seth's visor. "Your eyes seem to excite them. Can you stop them from glowing?"

Seth warded off another one. "Only with a pointy stick."

"Put your sun shield down," Nova advised when he pulled an especially tenacious specimen from his face. "And quit playing around."

The Naiyads drifted away once his eyes were obscured behind the shield. Nova turned her attention back to Caelyn and the creature in his hands. "So what's the story with the water ash here?"

"Some by-product of bacteria, possibly a waste product."

"Oh, great."

"It cycles through these oceans and is broken down by

sunlight. We have found no reason to believe that changing it with the catalyst will cause any problem for them."

"Well, let's get on with it," Seth said. "If we stay here much longer I'm going to sit down and never get up. I am already not too keen on leaving this place. Is this doing something to our heads?"

"Perhaps. I feel it, too."

"Nova?"

"Hmm?" she said, distracted by the glow of lights in the distance. "Oh, yeah. Let's do this." She waved her arms in a slow motion, watching the Naiyads waft out of the way as she moved. "That song keeps slowing down like it's going to stop and then I want to go that way."

"I don't recommend it," Caelyn said. "There is a trench that way. These Naiyads live down there, like a community or breeding grounds or hatchery. I don't really understand it. Let's just stay where we are." He walked over to her and took her arm. "Ready for this?"

"Not really."

He sealed the improvised valve around her arm and peeled back the sleeve, ensuring that no air escaped that way and to keep a tight pressure on her veins. One of the Naiyads had attached itself to his shoulder and watched with unblinking eyes.

"Seth..."

"I'm here," he said, his voice steady.

"Yeah, but you hate needles."

"I have the feeling there won't be any." He moved to stand behind her.

Her arm was now exposed to the Naiyad ocean and her skin tingled in response to the substance. The creature on Caelyn's shoulder slid down and moved over her arm. Like a wet sponge, it caressed her skin until she felt the edge of a sharp protuberance on one of the limbs. It sliced into her skin. Blood billowed into the surrounding fluid and Nova cried out in pain. The creature brushed over her again, opening another cut. Then a stinger dug into her arm as it had dug into her neck weeks ago.

Another Naiyad approached and also swiped at her. And another. Nova moaned in pain and stumbled backward, into Seth's arms. "It hurts, Seth." She had to fight the impulse to brush the creatures away from her skin.

"How much of this does she have to take?" Seth snapped at Caelyn.

"She'll know."

Nova bit her lip and forced herself to breathe in deep, measured inhalations. Long ribbons of blood moved through the amber liquid and then dissipated. Soon they perceived a change in their surroundings, much like the model in Celessa's lab. The color of the sea itself was transforming, moving outward from Nova's arm and ever faster as it accelerated in some chemical chain reaction that seemed to take only moments. The ceaseless song of the ocean faltered momentarily and then began again at a higher pitch that made Caelyn wince in pain.

She swooned, feeling the edges of her vision move in closer. Something seemed to be pulling the blood from her now as if the catalyst itself was looking to escape from her body. "It's alive," she whispered. "It knows."

"That's not possible!" Seth objected. He watched helplessly as yet another tentacle whipped across Nova's arm. "When are they going to stop?"

"They don't even know that this is hurting her."

"Well, tell them!"

"It's done," Nova said. "There is no more."

Seth turned her around and moved as quickly as the thick fluid allowed toward the shore. Caelyn followed and wrapped his arm around her from the other side when they lurched out of the sea and onto the dusty beach. Nova lolled between them, hardly aware of her surroundings.

Seth took a last look back over the smooth ocean and saw that the lace of water ash had turned a paler shade of amber.

They climbed into the *Dutchman*'s cargo bay. Seth raised the door and moved to the control panel. "All right, now let's hope this catalyst worked or this'll be a very short experiment." They waited for the decon process to remove the biological traces of Naiya from the exterior of their suits.

Caelyn shifted Nova to read the display on the wall. "It's not finding any ash," he said with just a trace of excitement in his voice. "It should be redlining by now."

Seth nodded and let the hold fill with oxygen-rich air. "Can I convince you to go first?"

This time Caelyn actually smiled. "Together."

Both men cringed in apprehension while they removed their helmets. Moments ticked by. The decon system alarms remained silent. No one choked. No one died.

Seth grinned when the ash clinging to their suits seemed to cause little more than an unpleasant urge to sneeze. "We did it. Nova, it worked!"

She raised a thumb, using the arm that still seemed to function. Then her knees buckled and she dropped to the floor. Caelyn and Seth discarded their suits and then peeled Nova out of hers. Her face was ghostly pale. "We have to get back to Trans-Targon," Seth said. "Now. She's lost so much blood!"

Caelyn opened the pressure door to the cabin. "I'm not sure I can do this now. Do you have a med box?"

Seth carried Nova inside and settled her into a chair. Her clothes were drenched in blood and more still seeped from the wounds on her arm. "That blue door there. Trauma kit hanging in the back. Check the date on the saline." He waited impatiently until Caelyn brought the box of medical supplies. "Nova! Don't go to sleep! Stay with us." The gauze he used to apply pressure to her arm immediately turned red.

"I'm here," she said dully. "Don't shout. Kind of queasy, though. And cold."

Caelyn checked her pulse and then inspected Seth's supply of emergency treatments. He selected a tab and prodded Nova into slipping it under her tongue. "That'll keep her on her feet for a while." He hooked the bag of fluid to a conduit running along the cabin ceiling and then pulled a blanket from lounger. "I'll get us ready for takeoff. No guarantees that we'll end up anywhere near this galaxy when we jump. My head is killing me."

"Well, we can't stay here," Seth said, shifting Nova to wrap the blanket around her. "Come on, Red. Sit up, lift your arm."

"Gonna throw up, I think," she said and drooped against him.

"Well, if you must." He nodded to Caelyn to go ahead into the cockpit. "We'll need you for this, Nova."

"I got some blood on me," she mumbled. "And you."

"A bit," he agreed. Her shirt and part of her breeches were smeared in a frightful, bloody display that made his own stomach a little uneasy, too. "But it's stopped now. You'll be fine. Keep pressing on this spot. We'll need you in the cockpit once we leave Naiya."

"Going back now?" Whatever it was that Caelyn had given her was beginning to make her feel better. "I wonder for how long they'll lock us up."

"Well, maybe we'll get lucky and Air Command lost the battle."

"You're a funny guy, Kada." She waved her hand toward the cockpit and noticed that her fingers had swollen to sausage proportion in reaction to Naiyad's ocean. "Don't let him get into trouble for us."

"Bah, civilian. Bloody Delphis do what they want, anyway," Seth said. "Isn't that right, Caelyn?"

"That's about right," Caelyn replied. "Would you like to leave now?"

Seth cast another worried glance at Nova before joining Caelyn in the cockpit. Skipping pre-flight procedures, he lifted off and hovered out over the sea before accelerating away from the planet. They watched it recede on their screens even as the *Dutchman* began to pry into the keyhole back to Trans-Targon.

Nova left the lounger, carrying her bag of fluid, and came to stand between the two pilot chairs. Her body still felt like it was made of pudding but she wasn't about to faint. "Can we do this?"

Seth looked up. "There isn't anything out here except Naiya, so we better. Naiya is remarkably short on air." His eyes shifted to Caelyn. "Counting on you, Delphi."

"Hold your end up, Centauri," Caelyn replied lazily.

"What can I do?" Nova said. "You have only the two interface sets."

"You can join us," Seth said with a questioning look to Caelyn. The Delphian nodded. "Why don't you take a seat on Caelyn here, and we can go for jump."

"What? *On* Caelyn?" she said when he took her hand and pulled her toward himself. She hooked her IV bag to where Seth normally kept the interface headset and climbed uneasily onto Caelyn's bench. She stretched out on his long body, guessing their intent. "This is awkward. And insane."

"No groping the Human, Caelyn," Seth said and settled into his interface.

"I'll behave. Emitters online. Go neg when ready."

Nova closed her eyes when the jumpsite to Trans-Targon opened before them and Caelyn used his link to the *Dutchman*'s processors to expand the breach and allow them to enter. She reached across the space between the chairs to take Seth's hand.

"See you on the other side," Seth said. "Hopefully."

Caelyn's fingers moved over her cheek and touched her neural node. She gasped when she perceived something, some presence in her mind that was more tangible than what she experienced when interfacing with a machine. "Whoa," she whispered. "Is that you?"

"Focus," he said. All three of them now used their link to each other and the processors to augment Caelyn's exhausted energies to direct the ship to the point in space they hoped to reach. Obediently, the *Dutchman* shot forward into the breach and their world disappeared.

* * *

Nova became aware of herself only a little while later. Her next awareness was of the Delphian's angular body beneath hers, then the muted noises from the dashboard. She lifted her head. Seth had dropped her hand and both men lay with their eyes closed, unmoving.

"Seth?" She blinked. "Oh, crap!" She slid from Caelyn's lap and groped for the manual controls. The *Dutchman* was tumbling wildly after having been spewed from the breach at the same speed it had entered and it took every bit of her skill and likely a fair bit of luck to bring it under control.

The ship shimmied unsteadily and Seth frowned as he opened his eyes. "Wha..?"

"We're back! He did it! But look at this."

He scanned the wide curve of the overhead screen, finding most of it taken up by a field of swiftly moving vessels. Cruisers, liftplanes, fighter ships of both Shrill and Kite classes spun and swooped around each other and the rebel station. A colossal Air Command carrier hovered in the distance, still issuing fighters. "Looks like your colonel got busy," he said.

The tactical system came online when someone in that melee targeted the *Dutchman*. Seth reached across the space between the pilot chairs and tapped Caelyn's arm. "Let the lady sit."

Caelyn groaned and opened his eyes which widened in dread when he saw the battle on the screen. "By the gods!" He stared, frozen to immobility even when the *Dutchman* shuddered under the assault of a well-placed missile.

"That's Air Command firing on us. Move!" Nova pulled on his arms when he finally stirred, barely conscious after having taken these two dangerous leaps through subspace. He lurched to the cockpit door and she took his place in the bench to link her neural interface to the ship's tacticals.

Seth began a series of swift evasive moves, looking for a pattern in this engagement. There was none. The rebel Shrills buzzed like angry insects around the platform, darting around each other as if for lack of direction. Some of the larger Shri-Lan cruisers hovered at a safer distance, taking shots at the Air Command ships flying in far more disciplined formation around them. Debris from destroyed vessels cluttered the space between the two forces, too fragmented to identify.

"I'm not going to get around that," Seth said with a curse when his attempt to move the periphery of the field was blocked by a military cruiser. "Those are Eagles. We need an opening."

Nova frowned at the flight path that now appeared, superimposed upon the battle. "Through there? That's Air Command. We can't just—"

Another hit slammed into the *Dutchman's* shields, and now an alarm whined above their heads.

"Us or them, Nova!"

Nova saw a squad veer left and head straight for the *Dutchman*. She placed her defensive fire before them, relieved when they were forced into evasive maneuvers.

"*Dutchman*," someone's voice reached them via their com. One of the rebel commanders had noticed their return to the station. "Quit evading. They're wide open over there. Take them out!"

"Aye, command," Seth replied, painfully aware that this transmission would be picked up aboard the Union carrier. He rolled again to get out of the way of the Kites. "Engaging."

A direct hit impacted against the *Dutchman's* portside shield.

"Nova!" Seth snapped. "Stop playing nice. We have to get out of here."

She ground her teeth and edged her fire closer to the Kites. One of them seemed to be in trouble and crossed a wingmate's flight path, perilously close to his team members and into Nova's line of fire. She cursed when her weapon grazed him and he spun away to break up at a safe distance from his squad. "One of ours, Seth! Gods, I hit one of ours."

"There's an Eagle after us," Seth said. Their sensors had

detected the high-end cruiser bearing down upon them, practically shouldering the smaller planes out of the way.

Nova redirected her fire and singed the Eagle's nose. These were Air Command's most highly trained pilots; surely they'd notice her deliberate avoidance of serious damage. They'd stand down to investigate. Maybe. But there was no time for guesswork when a pack of Shrills and Kites came between them. Recognizing Seth's ship as the greater threat, the Kites turned their attention on the *Dutchman*.

"I can't do this, Seth! Those are my people." She ignored his objections and redirected the *Dutchman*'s guns to target the rebel ships instead.

This felt right. This felt like things were supposed to happen. When the rebel Shrills fell to her aim, her mental focus maintained an unwavering grip on the ship's arsenal, deciding without fail the trajectory, enemy response, type of weapon, and conservation of resources to land one blow after another.

She opened the com. "Air Command, this is Lieutenant Nova Whiteside. Hold your fire."

"That worked so well last time you thought you'd try it again?" Seth said, ducking out of the way of another projectile.

She sent a rapid pattern of laser fire after an escaping rebel cruiser, noticeably avoiding the Air Command ship pursuing it. The Eagle fell back, perhaps confused by their behavior. By someone's command, the Kites returned to their chase of the Shrills, who were now fleeing without direction into empty space.

"I think they got it, Seth," she said. "They're moving off."

But then a missile from the Air Command carrier itself slammed pointblank into the *Dutchman*'s upper shield seam, placed there with precision by someone who knew their craft. Seth rolled the ship and shifted what few resources they had left to the generator. Something beeped somewhere below the floor of the cockpit and now a squawk from the com board announced some inquiry from someone nearby. Seth shut down a converter near the thorium storage. "The left crossdrive tanked. We're going nowhere now. Another one of those and we're gone."

She signaled their attackers again. "Lieutenant Whiteside to Air Command vessel. We surrender."

"Nova, this isn't—"

"Whiteside," a harsh military accent rang from the com. "Stand down all weapons and come about."

Seth's eyebrows rose and he pursed his lips. "Guess you do have friends in the army," he said.

Nova closed her eyes and exhaled forcefully. One by one, she peeled her cramped fingers from the armrests of her bench and then removed the neural interface.

The *Dutchman* obeyed Seth's commands to take the weapons offline. When he pulled the ship out of its evasive maneuvers, two Air Command cruisers braced them, weapons locked. "There goes my plan to outrun them to the next jumpsite."

"You might want to arrange for some repairs, first." Nova waved at the lively array of flashing warning signs on the console. She moved her arm when she noticed her blood had smeared the edge of the bench. "And maybe some light housekeeping."

"Dock immediately and prepare to be boarded," someone snapped at them over the com.

They ignored the voice but followed the order to approach the station, picking their way across the battlefield. Another Eagle cruiser hovered by the locks and just a handful of Shrills remained of the rebel fleet. A few Air Command Kites buzzed the area and sweepers already cruised the battlefield, scooping up bodies and valuables before they drifted too far. The massive Union carrier loomed nearby, dwarfing all in her shadow.

Nova came to her feet and turned to find Caelyn sprawled on the threshold of cockpit. She stepped over his legs and bent to peer into his face. "Caelyn? Are you in there?"

He accepted her help to rise and she once again deposited him in the co-pilot chair, doubting that she had the strength to heave him into the cabin and to the lounger.

"I'd like to be left alone now," the Delphian said in a tired murmur. "Please go away, both of you."

She smiled and kissed his forehead. She wasn't sure if Delphians engaged in forehead-kissing, but that wasn't about to stop her. "Thanks for getting us back."

Seth nudged the *Dutchman* into a lock on the platform. The connection was rough and Nova stumbled on her way to the cargo bay but the ship soon came to rest.

He powered down most of the ship's systems and joined her by the exit, wincing when he put his weight on his injured leg. "How are you holding up, Red?" he said, cradling her forearm in his hands to inspect the angry red welts among the deeper cuts.

"Not well. I killed a Union pilot today. He was just doing his job. I feel horrible."

"Not so much fun being a rebel, is it?"

"Have you done that?" she said. "Killed one of ours?" She raised her hands before he had time to object to her question. "Never mind. I'm not supposed to know. Hell, I don't really *want* to know."

His eyes remained on the livid rash on her arm for so long that she wondered if he'd reply at all. "You can't save everybody you like any more than you can just shoot everybody you don't," he said at last. "Collateral damage, either way." He smiled wistfully and nodded toward the *Dutchman*'s gate. "Let's get this over with, shall we?"

"Yes," she said resolutely. "I'm ready."

"For what?"

"They'll arrest you and then Baroch will find a way to cut you loose again. They'll arrest me and put me in front of a court martial. The best I can hope for is to get thrown out of Air Command. I don't have your kind of immunity."

"You could lie, you know."

"No, I can't. I killed a Union pilot. And Drackon's guard.

I'm a deserter. Disobeyed orders. Aided the enemy. Unlawfully at large. And I cost the Commonwealth a fortune in water ash."

"And you saved a few million sentients from a very dreadful future. I like that part best." He wrapped an arm around her shoulder and kissed her softly. "And being in hell with you. That was fun, too."

"Yeah, it was." She sighed. "I suppose I could get a job as a rebel."

He brushed a wayward strand of copper hair from her face. "You'd make a terrible rebel. What you are is a Union officer." He kissed her again. "Do you trust me?"

"With my life."

"Then trust me now." He leaned toward the door to drop the *Dutchman*'s gate. It lowered to reveal a dozen armed soldiers, guns aimed squarely at them. A few shifted uneasily when they saw the blood on Nova's clothes.

Seth grasped a fistful of her hair and raised a gun that she didn't even know he had been holding. He pressed it under her jaw and stepped out of the *Dutchman*. Nova cried out and tried to twist away, furious. His grip on her hair tightened painfully.

"Back!" he shouted. "Back off or the colonel's daughter is going to bleed a whole lot more."

The first row of soldiers retreated a few cautious steps to allow their senior officer to move forward. "You can't really think we'll let you leave," Colonel Carras said.

"Try me," Seth snapped back. "That cruiser on Three better be ready for takeoff by the time we get there."

"I'm warning you. Let the lieutenant go."

"But she is so much fun!" Seth leaned close to Nova and brushed his lips over her cheek. She glared angrily, still unable to move her head. "Now is a good time for you to escape, Red," he whispered into her ear and loosened his grip.

Nova raised both arms, clasped her hands and rammed her elbow deep into the pit of his stomach. A surprised grunt escaped him. She twisted and applied the very hand-to-hand combat maneuvers he had taught her so long ago in the halls of the academy. The years since then had given her much practice and he soon found himself on the floor, likely in a considerable amount of pain, her boot on his windpipe. "Move and I'll crush it," she hissed, as angry as she sounded.

He looked up at her with a sardonic smirk and managed a shrug. She stepped away when soldiers surrounded them to pull him to his feet. Seth was disarmed and bound and one of the men did not resist his urge to punch him with the grip of his gun. Nova winced Seth reeled backward from the blow.

"Get a medic," the colonel shouted over his shoulder.

"Kind of you, Carras." Seth wiped blood from his lip.

"Get him out of my sight." Carras scowled at the soldiers gripping Seth's arms. "I need him in shape to answer questions, so stand down."

"Colonel—" Nova began.

"Not a word out of you, Lieutenant." Carras glanced at the fresh blood seeping through her bandages. "Take her up to the Zoya."

EPILOGUE

"The last item on the agenda, I'm sure you're all glad to see, is one First Lieutenant Nova Whiteside." The Chair of the meeting peered at his screen without looking around to see if the subject of their inquiry was actually in the room.

Nova came to her feet and approached the designated spot in front of a semi-circle of seated officials. She had spent most of the day in this room, waiting her turn, alternately anxious and bored, hoping for the best, fearing the worst. Her current commanding officer sat in the gallery where she had spent most of the past few hours glaring at Nova in silent condemnation. At least she had not been called in front of the Board; this gathering was a sub-committee clearing a few outstanding cases that did not fall into the routines of other agencies. Still, these people were of the highest ranks and none of them looked particularly pleased with the last case on the roster.

She stood stiffly before this assembly of two Factors, a general and three colonels, Carras among them. One of the men sported a long braid of blue-black hair and she realized that this was Baroch, the Delphian Factor. Neither Drackon nor Rellius were in the room.

Colonel Denja finally looked up to examine the officer in front of him, scrutinizing the crisp gray uniform, tightly wound red hair and polished insignia as if he expected her to leap across the table to strangle him with her empty gun belt. The other officials were still poking at their screens. Had none of them read her case before showing up here today?

Finally the colonel seated next to Denja leaned over to murmur something. Her eyes went out over the seats in the back of the room.

Denja nodded. "Due to the nature of this case and its current classification, we ask that the gallery be cleared."

Nova did not turn to watch the officers and onlookers file out of the chamber, muttering among themselves, displeased by the announcement. Nova was not. One of the people leaving the room was her father.

Colonel Denja waited until the spectators had left and only the committee remained along with the clerk witness who was supervising the recording system for the session. "We assume that you have recovered from your... ah, abduction?" he said.

"Yes, sir," Nova replied. She had spent the last three weeks in Targon's hospital wing, most of that behind locked doors, while her case was scrutinized, sanitized and classified. After having endured a barrage of physical and psychological examinations she had been left alone until her fate was decided. "Thank you, sir."

They kept her standing at attention a while longer while consulting their reports. She cast a hopeful glance at Colonel Carras but he, too, was looking elsewhere. Only the Delphian Factor, Baroch, observed her with calculating intensity.

"We have read your deposition and so this is merely a formality," Denja said. "Your indictments against Colonel Sam Drackon and Factor Rellius are on record and, as you know, are under investigation. Your testimony, the video evidence, the colonel's presence on the rebel platform along with other corroborating evidence and statements is compelling. I can tell you that we have been able to confirm his involvement in several unauthorized diversions of Union resources. The Shri-Lan rebel facility on Aram has been routed and the sixteen hostages were liberated. Rellius is none of your concern."

"Yes, sir."

"Something troubles me," Denja said, scratching his chin as he deliberated. "I wonder why you, an Air Command officer, did not immediately report the assassination attempt on Targon to the base commanders." His gesture included Colonel Carras.

"Sir, I was unfamiliar with the base and have no trusted contacts there. The assassin mentioned a colonel and suggested further rebel operatives on Targon. I saw it necessary to remove myself from the situation until I could assess my options."

"With the help of Sethran Kada. A known rebel sympathizer."

"He had been cleared by Colonel Carras at that point, sir. I did not become aware of his true affiliations until after we had crossed into Magran space." She glanced at Factor Baroch and was certain that he had nodded with the barest tilt of his head.

"Should not have been cleared," Factor Coyle interjected, a sharp note in his voice. He looked down the table at his peers. "That man is a rogue!"

Factor Baroch replied with a meaningful glance toward Nova. Coyle sat back in his chair, looking far from mollified, but said no more. Nova suspected that Seth's name had come up at meetings such as this before today.

Denja studied his screen for a while and then addressed her again. "We have questioned Sethran Kada. Although we have contradictory statements, he insists that you were under duress and that you were forced to accompany him and the Delphian to Naiya. Shan Caelyn declined to make any statement regarding this matter other than to confirm that taking you there was the only way to cure you of this... affliction brought on by your exposure to the Myrid."

"Naiyad, sir," she corrected.

"Pardon?"

"They are called Naiyads. Myrids are indigenous to other regions of Trans-Targon."

He frowned and hummed for a moment before dismissing the irrelevancy. "In any case, Sethran Kada confirmed eyewitness reports that your involvement was not voluntary."

This time Nova caught Colonel Carras' eyes, surprised to see a hint of amusement on his face. Denja seemed to be engaged in verbal calisthenics to prevent her from perjuring herself. Neither he, nor anyone else, had asked her for her view about the 'abduction'. She dared to breathe a little easier.

"The loss of that planet to Commonwealth interests cannot be overstated," Denja continued. "But we understand that Kada's unorthodox attempt at protecting its native population likely prevented a catastrophe at the hands of Colonel Drackon."

Nova said nothing and waited through the long silence that followed.

At last, Factor Coyle leaned forward and folded his hands in front of him. "Lieutenant, there is no question in our minds that you did not use your best judgment when leaving Targon. However, given your past performance and record, we will be able to mitigate the damage this may have caused your career." He paused to direct another disgruntled glance at Factor Baroch. "Indeed, because of some of the principals involved, the incident is classified and will remain sealed outside the requirements of the ongoing investigation. You will retain your current rank and none of this will appear on your records."

Nova released a long breath and dared to relax her tensed shoulders. "Sir, if my relationship to Colonel Whiteside is influencing the decision of the Council, I wish to—"

"However," Coyle interrupted. "We feel that it is in your best interest that you are reminded of the chain of command

and the value of military protocol and practices. You are a pilot and your mission is to eliminate enemies of the Union. Your personal feelings about that are irrelevant and you are not required to *think* outside the mandate of your rank. You lost sight of your mission. We don't need anarchists in our organization, no matter how useful they appear at times. You will report to Colonel Yates on Ud Mrak as soon as your transport can be arranged."

Nova felt her jaw tighten at this censure but her face remained immobile. The lawless Mrak system, where the unexplored Badlands met the Trans-Targon sector, included two planets relying on Air Command to keep the peace. As on places like Bellac and even Magra, rebel factions harried their flanks and local politics forced the Union into taking sides. But, Nova consoled herself, she would be back in a fighter plane where she belonged.

She remained standing while the committee concluded its business and filed out of the room. Since her father was waiting for her outside she was not especially eager for them to hurry. At least she would not have to discuss the now-classified events of these past few weeks with him. She turned when she felt a heavy hand on her shoulder.

"I must say that went in your favor, Whiteside," Carras said, a mellow gleam in his violet eyes.

"It stung a bit but thank you, Colonel. For everything."

"No one wants to see your career compromised, Lieutenant. We've gained much here, even with the loss of Naiya and the disappearance of Pe Khoja. Of course you know that this is serving the Union as much as it does you. Drackon's actions are, to say the least, embarrassing. Your... involuntary presence in this case has helped to uncover far more than expected."

"Rellius?"

"Yes, Rellius. You've likely seen a side of our fine Air Command we prefer to keep in the dark, but I believe I can rely upon you to keep our little secrets." Carras chuckled, amused by his understatement.

"To be honest, Colonel, I'm... troubled, I guess, by what seems like a whole lot of—"

He raised a hand to cut her off in mid-sentence. "You can make a choice, Lieutenant. Do as Factor Coyle advised and don't think. Take what they're offering and walk away. Or you can accept that none of us know the way of running this vast organization without... compromises. Some of those compromises are not what you and I might find fair or even ethical. And sometimes we need to do what we can to keep ourselves in check, as you found out." He lowered his voice. "My advice is to forget what Factor Coyle said. Never stop thinking. You are not a drone. I'm going to keep my eye on you. I have a hunch we'll make good use of your talents in the future."

"I hope so, sir," she said, sounding far from convinced.

"And perhaps I can hope you will come to trust me should you find yourself in trouble again, Lieutenant, rather than rely on, well, outside help."

"Yes, sir."

Carras scanned the empty chamber for a moment before his eyes settled on her again. "Something in the classified reports still puzzles me, Whiteside. You stated that you shot Colonel Drackon in self-defense using a stun gun."

"I did, sir. He was firing at Shan Caelyn. He was subsequently incapacitated."

The colonel nodded thoughtfully. "So you reported. But when Drackon was found, some of his injuries were not consistent with merely having been stunned."

She raised her eyebrows. "Sir?"

"Nor were they consistent with a fall. In fact, judging by several burns he sustained it would appear that he was subjected to direct contact with the same class of weapon. A painful and controversial technique, I'm sure you are aware, of gaining compliance."

"Oh," she said. "I have no knowledge of anything that happened to him after we left the cell block."

"Without Sethran Kada."

"Correct, sir. He joined us later."

"And subsequently unearthed a remarkable amount of information regarding the colonel's activities over the past five years. Or, rather, Factor Baroch came into possession of this information."

"I would not know about that, sir," she said. "I suppose the colonel would have a considerable amount of intelligence regarding Rellius."

"Which he has not disclosed to us in our own interviews."

She bit back a grin. "Sethran Kada can be... persuasive." She hesitated a moment. "Colonel, may I ask what happened with him?"

Carras hummed to himself for a while. "Kada? He is no longer in our custody. Perhaps that's all you need to know. I meant what I told you before. He is not someone you want to be associated with."

"Yes, I think you're right." She gazed into the middle-distance for a moment. Of course he was right. She had come to that conclusion over these past few weeks, thinking back and looking ahead. And Seth had known it, too. "I *know* you're right. But did... did he ask about me?"

The Centauri paused again. "Well, he did ask me to give you a message. I'm not sure it's appropriate."

"What did he say?"

"Hmm, I admit I'm a bit baffled by it, but he said, and these are *his* words, that he will see you in hell."

Nova laughed, no doubt baffling the colonel a little more. "I'm sure he'd like that."

* * * * *

*

ABOUT THE AUTHOR

Chris Reher is a first generation Canadian currently and out of necessity residing on planet Earth (which, in the general and interplanetary scheme of things, could *really* use a catchier name. Imagine heading past Proxima Centauri and someone asks you whence you came and you tell them "dirt". All theological implications aside, that just won't do.)

When not finding ways to defy the laws of physics or torture her subjects or entice them with inter-species hanky-panky, she designs web sites or writes about designing web sites. She enjoys long walks on the beach or, given the local beach shortage, writes about beaches far beyond Proxima Centauri.

www.chrisreher.com

By Chris Reher

Sky Hunter

The Catalyst

Only Human

Rebel Alliances

Delphi Promised

Quantum Tangle

Terminus Shift

Entropy's End

Made in the USA
Middletown, DE
16 August 2016